A RURAL ODYSSEY

Living Can Be Dangerous

MARK J. CURRAN

Order this book online at www.trafford.com
or email orders@trafford.com

Most Trafford titles are also available at major online book retailers.

Print information available on the last page.

ISBN: 978-1-4907-9584-3 (sc)
ISBN: 978-1-4907-9585-0 (e)

Trafford rev. 07/02/2019

www.trafford.com
North America & international
toll-free: 1 888 232 4444 (USA & Canada)
fax: 812 355 4082

SETTING THE SCENE

It's been eighteen years now, but wherever you begin, it's not going to happen again. It will never be the same for us. And I have a feeling it will never be the same for my people and my generation. I hope not, at least the way it ended. I write this not so much as a document of those times, but to force myself to remember them, to cherish them. I think something beautiful has passed and I doubt it will ever be the same again.

I remember you could go out the back door of the farmhouse, north across the yard and through the gate in the fence beside the chicken house, then through the windbreak which used to be empty ground and into the pasture. The grove of trees beyond the windbreak isn't there anymore, and for that matter, most of it is gone now. Things you don't figure will ever be gone. Then you realize what has happened. They were funny trees with funny bark. They had long black pods with smooth shiny seeds. We called it "the coffee bean tree." You went through the grove, and then there was only buffalo grass, thick, and it smelled good. Then you walked a quarter of a mile up the gradual slope to the bare spot on the low hill. You were tired by now and a little thirsty. So, you sat down to rest and looked back …

It was to my mind the prettiest view in the entire valley, summer or winter. The people in town kept their airplanes up here on the hill during the '51 flood. The valley was almost totally covered with Smokey Hill River muddy water then. But now you could see the green fields, dark green alfalfa down by the highway, corn that hadn't tasseled out yet and next to it and in nearby fields the wheat beginning to turn. You could hear the trucks coming along old U.S. highway 40 almost before you saw them. Hear the hum of the tires. And you knew a lot of the cars that went by, farmers down the road, the M.D. everyone thought was uppity and not really a farmer whose farm had the pretty white rail fence facing the road and Thoroughbreds behind the fence. The farm across the highway was pretty, completely flat with good soil. Beyond it the railroad tracks. The trains that came through there! They caused more than one fire at harvest time. That was before the diesels. You heard them at night with a cool southeast breeze and the wail of that whistle. Good dreams.

To the southwest of the hill was the gradual slope in the pasture, then the farm house, farm buildings and barnyard; a bit south of that yet was the farm across the highway with the Johnson's dairy, beyond that the outline of the city hospital, and the good buddy's place. I used to cut across the fields on Sunday afternoon to the Zimmermans for ball games and talk and home-grown popcorn. Later on, I rode a bike on the highway up the hill and by the hospital. You could made out the buildings on the edge of town pretty well, but most clear were the alfalfa mill and the grain elevator.

So, the view was nice, as nice as any around in the central Kansas flatlands. Looking down that hill gave me the feeling you hear about, thinking "This is mine." Even if it wasn't, it felt good to know my Daddy owned it. You could look down and see the windbreak with the cedars, walnut and other trees that were all planted from scratch and watered with the buckets of water by my Dad. On the other side of the windbreak were the low chicken house with the tin roof, the two-story granary to its right, then the silo and corral. Beyond the silo was the great old barn with the old-fashion loft and all that goes with it. The water tank for the livestock and the hog house were on the other side of the barn. The house was best, a two-story frame with an attic and basement. Asbestos on the sides when the hundred-year-old boards began to go, but with the great front porch where you could sit on a summer evening and watch the activity down the road and hear the trains coming.

At the top of the hill there were two lone trees and what we called the dump, really a shallow hole in the ground. That was where we took the unburnable trash, old fence wire, about anything we didn't need ended up there. It made the best place for a rabbit to hide, and consequently we headed there first when hunting cottontails or jack rabbits. From the two trees, practically the only ones in the north 80 which was all pasture, you could see to the north the county road marking the north end of the section and the 80. In the late 1950s the government took forty acres in the name of progress to build the Interstate. It's a nice four lane highway, but the view, the 80 and especially the water drainage down into our pasture and pond have never been the same since. It was great fun watching with my brother Paul all the big earthmoving equipment, the Caterpillars and graders when they were building it. And I learned a lot about Eminent Domain. And progress.

The east part of the north 80 was rough pasture. It had a good stand of brome grass and was baled regularly. There was a county gravel road along the east side of the farm. But the best part lies in between the road and the top of the hill with the dump and rabbits. We call it the pond. It isn't really a pond since there isn't any water in it most of the time, not since the highway went through. But once it was the best of all possible ponds with huge umbrella shaped shade trees, many birds about, and lots of water in the rainy years, enough for my Dad to stock some small bass and channel cats. And there were huge mosquitoes. But mainly it was trees. Trees planted by the hands of my father and watered by buckets and barrels of water he brought one by one from the well about a hundred yards away. All kinds of trees, trees I don't even know the name of. But mainly Black Walnut trees. For walnut fudge of course, and to feed the squirrels.

The pond was a player for a while in local history, especially when you hear about swimming, overnight camping out with no sleeping bag, just a blanket on the ground, and later on a couple of notorious beer blasts. I had the entire freshman football team out for a bonfire with hot dogs and a fair amount of Coors donated by brother Paul from the pool hall. The pond was one of my favorite places to go. When I was a little guy it was inhabited by Iroquois Indians and later on by other types of "varmints and sidewinders." They didn't stand a chance when challenged by the 22-single shot.

To the south of the pond, all the way back down to old Highway 40 was the plowed land where most of the work took place. I covered most of it myself on a little Ford tractor, not by my own will, but covered it just the same. I can remember what was planted where, how it did, how it was rotated, where the muddy spots were during the plowing, where the rocky spot was up on the side of the hill. I had favorite fields, generally the ones near the highway so I could see friends go by on their way into town. I remember the patrol cars of the police ad even their airplanes the day of the great Enterprise bank robbery. More local history.

At the end of the rectangle I'm trying to make was the lane leading from the old highway up to the house, barnyard and corral. The lane had an alfalfa field on one side and a small field in brome grass to the west. My first excursions into that latter field are foggy notions of brome grass as tall as me, huge sunflowers in the corners and the small forest of trees down by the highway. Reginald Ross's big Chevy sign, the farm jungle gym, was planted in that corner as though it were to produce in the spring. There were times when I was slashing through the jungle of sunflowers and weeds with my machete and the wilds of Africa and South America were part of Dickinson County.

The lane was about one hundred yards long, give or take a few, straight and true all the way to the house. I traveled it at least twice a day for nine months of the year during the school year and once the rest of the year to get the paper and mail, all together for close to twelve years. It had three trees, two of them old and noble cottonwoods. You could always hear the leaves whir in the wind. The third was a dinky one, not worth much except to break the monotony of the walk. From the front porch of the farmhouse you could see clearly all the way down the lane and the mailbox at the end of it. The paper came all the way from Kansas City; the mail, the school bus from the Abilene Public Schools and the Easter Bunny candy eggs in season provided the reasons for being of that road and my memories. Best of all about the lane was the walk on a cool summer evening. Birds along the way, beetles in the ruts (we blew them up with firecrackers on the 4th of July), gophers and their mounds along the alfalfa on the right, and especially the view of the yard of the old house at its end.

1

THERE'S A REASON

There's a reason I'm telling this when I'm eighteen.

I'm Mick O'Brien and this is the story of how I grew up and all that happened. Dad was in his late 40s when I was born in 1941 (the kids at school teased about how old Mom and Dad were); he was born in 1893 up in Nebraska. Mom had me at age 40, a risky thing at her age then, in fact risky to the point that I was born an "incubator" baby at three pounds in the local community hospital. There's more to it: I was a twin; brother Mark did not make it. Mom would never talk about it much but just said, "It was a tiny thing of a hospital, a country hospital, they did everything they could." A couple of years later Mom was in the hospital in a bigger place, nearby Salina, for a "mysterious" operation; no one would explain it to me. It had to be a hysterectomy. No more kids.

Brother Paul was fifteen years older than I, really a half-brother from Mom's first marriage, more on that later. Sister Caitlin was five years older. Brother Joe was four years older. So, I'm the baby of the family; I think it got me some privileges and maybe a few spankings. I never thought our names were unusual but would learn later we were all with accustomed Irish names. It figures: Dad was Sean O'Brien and Mom Maureen "Molly" Ryan.

So, you might figure we were Catholic, a real minority in those parts. I don't think most people, and most were not well read in History and book educated, had ever gotten over Rome and the Pope (a joke was: "Does a bear shit in the woods? Is the Pope a Catholic?") We were the "cat lickers." The town had just 7000 people and twenty-seven churches in the telephone directory. You would see the River Brethren ladies in the black bonnets and full skirts in town, the men in black hats, mainly for trading time on Saturday. It was big time Bible Belt, but I don't think I realized it then. I remember all the public schools being dismissed I think around Christmas time for a Jesus movie down at the Plaza Theater. I don't think any of this every made much difference to me, I was too busy having fun, getting into trouble now and again and just being a boy. Now I suspect there was a lot that wasn't said.

2

KINDERGARTEN, THE FARMHOUSE, LUKE

It's 1946 and I'm only five, getting ready to go to Kindergarten at Garfield School in Abilene. My hair is combed (for a change) and I'm wearing a sort of bib-short with white socks and leather shoes. I'm clean, not a spec of farm dirt on me. I'm told to hurry up by brother Joe, he's half out the farm house door, sister Caitlin is already down the lane. We can't be late for the little yellow school bus, it don't wait for no one.

I figure you might be interested in what I remember then. I was told I was smart and must have a good I.Q. I'm not sure what that means, but I sure do have a good memory. I'm already reading, and I tend to talk a lot, sometimes it's "smart alecky" talk, and ends up with a spanking. I know the feeling of Dad's hand and even his leather belt on my butt. And I can't remember a time when we were not reading at home and would go weekly to the town library and check out the maximum number of books, for me lots of science fiction and anything to do with a trip to the moon.

Our house was two-story with an attic and cellar. I can scarcely remember but have foggy notions of a coal stove in the middle of the kitchen, running water from a well, and electric lights. The bathroom was a busy place with six people needing to use it, all unscheduled. You just banged on the door, hollered "Hey I've got to go" and hoped someone

3

would come out soon. If they didn't you had another recourse: the old wooden outhouse to the north of the house, a two- hole. I do remember that place, most often for some reason in the springtime, sitting with the door open, contemplating the garden in front of it, the alfalfa field beyond that and the corn field way off to the east. Most of the time I was preoccupied in not getting bit by a spider; there were webs all over the place. I was told we didn't have Black Widows but that there were Brown Recluses. Enough to send shivers up your spine. So, you did your business and got the hell out of there. Oh, pardon my language, even in grade school you pick up what you hear, and my country cousins on the school bus are champions at swearing and bad grammar. Mom spent a fair amount of time correcting my "aint's" and "ain't gots" at the dinner table.

So I guess the main thing is I did get the Saturday night bath and was clean that day for the first day of school. Caitlin was supposed to get me to the door. It must have gone okay. School was just a half day, but we still got graham crackers and milk and this shiny vitamin pill to be washed down, all this before lying down on our "blankie" for a nap. All I remember is lots of giggling, both by the little guys like me and the cutie girls. Home again was the bus ride. You had to be sure and be ready to get off, Harry the driver seemed to know who was and who was not supposed to get off, so if it took a minute or two, it was okay. The bus had a round yellow sign to the side - "stop" - and most people did. I had to cross the highway and then walk up that long lane. Mom had cookies and milk waiting for the hungry five-year-old.

It was about that time, after school one day, that Mom said we needed to go over and meet the new neighbors, the Zimmermans from Oklahoma. They lived on a farm just east of the Abilene city limits, across from the hospital. I'm just a little guy, but I remember driving into their barnyard, Mom going up to the door to meet Sheila Zimmerman, and a bit later this little guy, turns out to be my age, coming out and saying "hi" in the front yard. I'm sure we didn't have too much to say, but Luke, that was his name, would go on to be probably my best friend growing up. There were lots of reasons: you could cut across the fields from our farm to theirs for play and sports, Luke was with me all those years in the Abilene schools, with me in sports in summer baseball and early school sports, but mainly, a constant buddy at church. We were all Catholics so that meant Catechism on Saturday morning, church on Sunday and a whole bunch of other times during Lent, Catholic Summer School, and being altar boys together at about age 12. Oh yeah, and I did farm work for Luke's dad Arnold during teen years.

3

MODERN APPLIANCES ON THE FARM

About this time, when you are a little kid like me on the farm, there's a lot you just sort of remember in a fuzzy way. That's the way it is with any appliances in the kitchen or bathroom or whatever.

I can't recall when I saw my first automatic clothes washer and dryer, maybe at the RHV store in town in the mid-1950s. But I do remember the new washer Dad got for Mom perhaps still in the late 1940s or early 1950s. It looked like some kind of spaceship from the early Jules Verne books, a round tub on four long legs with a small roller under each wheel, and the wringer, a hand-cranked contraption up above. I do not know what this machine replaced, but we did have the old wash boards (which hillbilly bands use for a funny percussion instrument). Somewhere way back I think I recall Mom with the galvanized wash tub all full of soap suds with the wash board in it, scrubbing away. A more accurate memory of the tub was that we used it upon occasion to cool watermelons during the hot months of July and August. The scene comes back today: out on the old concrete back "stoop" with cool well water in the tub and a great big green watermelon ever so slowly being cooled.

And that makes me think of the old wooden crank ice cream maker that was used during the same weather. (I will talk about it out on the front porch on a summer evening when Mom tells her story.) Dad and Mom bought salt and ice in town, thick cream, and would make the ice cream on a hot evening in summertime. It seemed like it was always vanilla, but we absolutely loved it. However, our less than efficient electric refrigerator (we all called it the "icebox") and its freezer would not freeze it solid; but it did not seem to matter because it just tasted so good. My favorite part was getting to lick the beaters.

I'm still thinking about the old washing machine. Even with the new device, the time spent washing for four, five or six people is incredible, particularly when you think of the dirt from farm work and the clothes we peel off after a hot day in the fields. But the drying is the part I remember more because we don't have any automatic dryer, and everything has to be taken outside to the clotheslines located just north of the kitchen. One of my chores growing up is to help take out the clothes and hang up for drying, but more often to go out and get the clothes, put them in old wooden baskets (the same ones peaches and apples come in from the store) and bring them into the house. The matter is complicated to no end in wintertime; I can recall many times bringing in blue jeans stiff as a board from freezing overnight. Mom would iron them quickly, trying to dry them out some, but I can recall often going to school with very cool, wet shorts particularly from the pocket area and the crotch of the still wet jeans. I can also recall bed sheets frozen overnight.

My Mom is a very tiny lady, perhaps five feet tall at most and weighing not much over one hundred pounds. The physical energy it takes for the washing, the drying on the line, and then the ironing of clothes for six just overwhelms me. Mom is typical of her times and peers; the farm ladies work as hard as their men. With cleaning, washing, cooking and being the "nurse" and "doctor" to all of us, no wonder Mom seems to be worn out a good deal of the time. She'll say, "I'm so tired." It kind of hurts me inside then.

The other electrical appliances in the farmhouse are up to date (for the 1940s): a modern electric stove, refrigerator, electric hot water heater, a mixer for blending, electric iron, and a vacuum cleaner (I cannot remember the brands, but a "Hoover" I think). But there is no blender, no automatic dish washer, no garbage disposal (except for the Collie dogs and diverse cats swarming outside the porch door after meals), and certainly no microwave, all these we will see on TV ads come 1955. And little help to boot. Although Caitlin has learned to cook well and sew well from her Mother, it's Mom who prepares most of the meals and does the necessary sewing. No wonder she is tired and worn out so often. The kids are enlisted to help with dishes, and I do a lot of drying and banging them around.

Ah, the telephone. Things are a bit different now when I'm writing this. Ours originally was the wall mounted variety with the receiver hanging on a hook from the main wooden box containing the mouthpiece and innards of the thing. There was a crank on the right side to turn in order to get the operator. Ours was, like most everyone else's then, a party line. So I think our "number" was signaled by a long and two shorts from the bell. We became familiar with the "ring" for the neighbors as well, so you would know who was being called, and when you picked up the receiver to make a call, likely as not, there was someone already on the line. At some point, I think I was well into junior high or high school, the telephone company replaced the old phone with a desk model, no crank involved, but the party line continued for some time. Being not quite a saint, I will admit I did listen in a bit, but just a bit. But when you were talking there were always these mysterious "clicks" letting you know someone had been listening in to your own conversation.

Radio and then television in 1955 were the most fun and added totally different dimensions to our lives in rural Kansas.

4

DAD, PART ONE, NEBRASKA

Dad didn't talk much, especially at 6:00 p.m. sharp when Gabriel Heater was on the tabletop radio on the kitchen counter near the supper table. He would thunder, "Listen!!" No one talked then. But there were other times when he was always ready to answer my questions. One of those times he put me on his lap after supper and I asked, "Dad, where did we all come from? I just remember seeing a picture of me sitting on brother Paul's lap at the house on Brady street in Abilene, me with long curls and blond hair. How come now we're on a farm?"

"Mick, it's a long story and maybe you're old enough to remember some of this. We O'Briens came from Ireland in the 1840s, in the beginning in Ohio my grandad worked in the coal mines along with his brothers and a lot of relatives. But we were all originally farm folks in Ireland; I understand from my Dad (I never knew my grandad) that we were part of that potato famine. Do you know what "famine" is? It's being hungry with nothing to eat. Our main crop was potatoes but there was a blight and the crops failed; the damned English hoarded their food and money. We were told if you want to survive, get the hell out of Ireland and go to America. We'll be glad to be rid of the whole lot of you. I don't know exactly how that all was arranged, but only that we ended up in Ohio. But farming was in our blood and a love to live on the land and make a living from it.

9

"My Dad and his brothers and a whole passel of us Irish made a big move to southeast Nebraska, must have been the 1860s. We were sponsored by some wealthy Irish, I think the Ryans who had homesteaded near Dawson, and they loaned my Dad and others the money to make the trip West. I figure it must have been by horse and buggy, but the trains were being built then and lots of Irish were laborers driving spikes into the ties. Anyway, my Dad was able to rent a quarter section, this because his sister Amy was a domestic for the Ryan family and Mr. Ryan wanted to help her out. Enough for now, time for your bedtime."

5

THE FARMHOUSE THE STOCK TANK AND A CLOSE CALL, AND LATER, FISTICUFFS AND BLUEJAYS

Mom was saying her Rosary in front of the heat register in the dining room, stopped and kissed me goodnight and said, "Sweet Dreams. Don't let the bedbugs bite." I don't know if that made any difference in my getting to sleep, but her prayers to the Virgin Mary continued. She was always talking about Our Lady of Fatima and we had to pray for the conversion of Russia. I didn't really understand all that but knew that Rosary would take place every night.

She would be in that same place every night. Maybe this is a good place to talk a little about the farmhouse. To the north with a north window was the kitchen with an electric stove, an old refrigerator (which we called the "ice box") and a breakfast nook where we actually could all fit in for meals except the big Sunday dinner in the dining room. The latter had a big antique wooden bureau on one side and the dining room table in the center. Aside from meals it also served as a card table; we played a lot of Gin Rummy and Mom and Dad would play pinochle and bridge with farm neighbors. My main memory about all that is directions: Dad would say, "Get me the newspaper, it's on the south side of the table." One funny memory was the time some Solomon relatives visited on a Sunday afternoon and one of the Callahan uncles from Solomon sat in a rocker in the dining room. When he left there was a wet ring of chewed cigar in a perfect circle around the rocker. Country cousins?

The living room faced the front porch and the lane to the highway. It had an old divan where lots of naps took place, an easy chair or two and a TV courtesy of brother Paul in 1955. That changed our lives.

The southeast corner of downstairs was the music room. There was an old upright piano, not in tune most of the time, music stands for Caitlin and her violin and Joe and his trumpet. When I started guitar later on, I would sit on the piano bench and prop my music up on the piano. And Mom had her Singer sewing machine in there. So it was a busy place.

I slept in one of the five bedrooms upstairs in the farmhouse, sharing a bed with brother Joe. For a while that is. I was a bed wetter, and even though there was a rubber sheet under the other bedding, all too often I couldn't hold it, or maybe was too lazy to make the trek down to the bathroom. And watermelon in the summer nights didn't help. Sometimes I just peed out the east window of the bedroom, through the screen. Always wondered why that didn't rust out. Joe moved out of desperation to Paul's room, vacated when he joined the Army-Air Force and was still training in Florida during World War II.

There was a hallway and then the stairway downstairs with a bannister. When I was little I always slid on the bannister down to the next level and then pounded down the stairs two at a time to the living room. A memory is all hearing – you knew who was coming up or down stairs by the sound of their footsteps, everybody was different. For some reason I remember Paul's most. And you could open a tiny window on the south end of the upstairs hallway and I would crawl out the window, sit on the porch roof, and listen to the birds and just look to see what was going on down the lane and the highway.

I was only about six when Paul came back home on one of those troop trains, a steam train. I remember because I could always hear the trains and their whistles at night from the east window of the bedroom. Lots of times I fell to sleep listening to them. Good dreams. Later on, I would realize it wasn't all good – their sparks would start fires in the wheat fields south of our farm. It was good news for me seeing Paul is his slick Army-Air Force uniform with that hat with the Air Force star in the middle, but not so good for Joe. He had to move back in with me.

It was about that time after Paul came home when I damned near died. I was just maybe five years old. It was the middle of winter, freezing temperatures and snow. One of my play games was to go down to the stock tank just south of the barn and "ice skate" on the ice. I just had farm boots on, but you could slide around and have fun. This time the ice cracked, and I fell through, probably just up to my waist. I started screaming at the top of my lungs. God knows how, maybe it was a miracle, Paul heard the screams, came running out of the house, across the driveway and down to the stock tank. He yanked me out of the ice and toted me back up to the warm farmhouse, carrying me like a sack of chicken feed or a bale of hay at his side. I was shivering in the middle of the kitchen; he and Mom pulled my boots off, my wet clothes and wrapped me in blankets and put me in front of the heat register. After a while I began to get warmed up, and then heard Mom say, "That was too much of a close call, Mick. I think you had better find other games to play. No more 'ice skating.' As Grandma would say, 'This is a fine kittle of fish.' You can thank Paul for hearing you. I don't know if it was the luck of the Irish, but thanks be to God he got you out of there. You better remember this when you say your prayers tonight." Paul just smiled and said, "Little brother, you're a pain in the rear end but I still love you."

There always seemed to be something happening. What's a boy to remember? I got in trouble in second grade when old mean, Miss Hansen caught me tracing my pencil on the wood carving already on my desk. Hell, it was already there; I was just making it prettier. But that was a time

I'll never forget how mean a teacher can be. For some reason one of my buddies got in trouble with her, she made him stay in for recess, and when we came back in, he was sitting in his chair crying, a puddle of pee on the floor. You remember the old "number 1" and "number 2" and one or two fingers up in the air when you couldn't hold it anymore? Why in hell she didn't let him go I'll never know. But I've never forgotten her.

More such stuff. It's all pretty foggy to me. But there was one moment, by now I'm in the third grade in old, mean Miss Winthrop's class. I was not her favorite student by far but did luck out for the class play that year. It was something to do with nature, so we were all dressed up as flowers, or if you were more better, birds. I got to be a Blue Jay and was dressed from head to toe in paper-blue feathers with a hat with a Blue Jay's tuft on top and even a beak. I remember I was supposed to walk across the stage and make bird sounds. Afterwards, still strutting my stuff in that suit, a classmate named Jimmy came up to be and socked me in the jaw. I still don't know why, maybe he didn't get to be a bird, but it hurt like hell. He muttered, "You dumb shithead. Mick, you're a 'Mick' and we don't like your kind much. Next time **I'm** going to be the bird and you'll be picking up my bird shit off the floor." He was a lot bigger than me, so I just tried to get over the pain in my jaw, this at home when Mom put a hot washcloth on it, saying, "Mick, I'm so sorry. There will always be bullies at school and these things happen." (She always had some kind of a saying to explain things.) I said, "I know my real name is Michael and it's just short by Mick, but what is a 'Mick'?" Mom hesitated some, I guess trying to think what to say, but after a bit said, "Mick, 'Mick' is a bad nickname for any person who happens to be Irish-American." "Do you mean like 'nigger'?" "Well, not so bad, and by the way that's the last time I want to hear that word in this house. There are a lot of us Irish here in Abilene, and we're all Catholics, and some of the people who don't like Negroes don't much like Catholics either. So maybe you should learn how to protect yourself. Joe is four years older than you and is stout and he knows how to punch. Take a few lessons from him."

So that next day Joe and I were out in the back yard, him trying to teach me how to box, to protect myself and maybe throw a punch or two. I don't know where he got the boxing gloves, maybe from the Sears – Roebuck catalogue. In the process I got a bruised chin and a black eye. He said, "You ain't exactly Jack Dempsey, but we'll practice some more and see if you get better." "Not soon enough for me," I said, rubbing my chin. It would be a few years before all that would pay off. Joe wasn't always so helpful. Dad still ran the cream station at the Union Pacific tracks downtown, and one time Joe was teasing me about something and I started crying and ran out the door of the cream station. I still don't know what that was all about, but I was mad. Another one of my shenanigans, but I had a temper. I could throw a tantrum as well as anybody and more than once told Mom I was going to run away. I would put some stuff in a big red kerchief, tie it to a stick and head off down the farm lane. I think I got the idea from a "Little Rascals" cartoon in the movies. By the time I got to the mailbox I was calmed down and remembered which side my bread was buttered on and walked sheepishly back to the house. I never missed a meal; maybe that had something to do with it. Mom and Dad must have had me figured 'cause they just smiled and said "Welcome back."

6

THE CAR WRECK, GRANDMA, AND IT HURTS DOWN DEEP

About that time, still third grade I think in 1949, something a lot worse happened. One of our big treats was to get to go with Mom in the old Buick the 25 miles to Salina for shopping. Mom made most of her and Caitlin's clothes, working away on an old Singer Sewing Machine. She bought all her sewing supplies up at the nearest Singer shop in Salina. Caitlin, Joe and I got to go along. There was a Woolworth's five and dime right across the street and that's where we headed, each with a shiny quarter to spend. They had big bags of popcorn for a dime, bubble gum, root beer barrels and we spent the whole thing in a hurry. I liked the caramel apples and succeeded in getting all gummy and sticky.

We were on the way home, near a tiny town called New Cambria when it happened. I'm riding in the front seat in the middle, Mom is driving, and Grandma Minnie is right of me (Mom's mom Minnie Ryan). Caitlin and Joe are in the back seat. All I'm telling you is what they told me later in the hospital in Salina. Older brother Paul I think. The road between Salina and Abilene is that same old Highway 40 that goes by the farm. It's two-lane, and Mom was behind one of the big orange highway trucks. It slowed down and when Mom went to do the same, no brakes! She had no choice and had to make a quick decision, either veer to the right and probably roll the car with all of us in it (and there were no seatbelts) or try to go around. She did the latter, but a car was coming straight at us and she slammed head on into it. Cars didn't go very fast in those days, but 50 miles per hour was enough.

I'm in the Catholic Hospital in Salina. Paul is in the room with me, Dad and Caitlin and Joe would be coming later. It isn't supposed to be funny, but Paul gets one of those small mirrors and holds it up to my face. My face is almost entirely black with stitches. For some reason it's funny. The blackest I had ever been. The strange thing is I'm in no pain. I had gone through the front windshield of the Buick and got a fractured skull. I guess that's why all the stitches. And I have a broken arm. But no pain. Paul then shows me my old favorite jacket, one of those made of material, maybe felt, but with leather strips in front. It's stiff and caked with blood. Paul goes on, "Mick, I think the fact you are alive is a miracle. They have been doing vigils and rosaries and prayer services for the last week at home at church at St. Andrew's praying for you. Any many other churches have joined in they tell me. Our prayers have been answered; you're going to make it."

That's when Dad, Caitlin and Joe came in. All of a sudden, I remembered (the accident itself and all later was blacked out for me) – "What about Mom and Grandma?" It was Dad who said, "Your Mom's been hurt, but she is going to mend. She had several broken ribs from hitting the steering wheel, her shoulder thrown out of place, and lots of bruises. We'll take you down to her room in just a few minutes. Mick, Grandma didn't make it; she went through the windshield as well. She's up in heaven looking down on you."

It was then I burst into tears and felt a grief that I can hardly describe. It hurt, deep down, not just in my head but everywhere. Grandma. I cried and cried, like never before (those bruises from fights were never like this). Dad added, "Mick, we had that St. Cristopher medal pinned to the car inside above the rear-view mirror. I'm sure he was watching over us all. Your Mom's going to be okay in a few days, Caitlin and Joe never had a scratch, probably because of that big stuffed front seat, and you're going to be released we think in about a week. Do you think you can go see Mom?"

After a while they wheeled me down to her room down the hall. The nurses were all nuns but in hospital clothes. When I saw her, all taped up and looking tired and wan I broke into tears again; the nun said, "She's pretty sore so you can't hug her yet." I remember a small detail; Mom had her rosary in her hand and smiled at me. "Mick, we'll all be better soon. We'll miss Grandma, God knows, but we'll be better. You are too young to understand but I have to tell you. I did my best. It all was the brakes on the car." I muttered, "Mom, I know, I understand, please get better." The next few days they would roll me into her room for the meals and put my bed in her room as well. We both got out of the hospital together. My arm was still in a cast, but they had pulled the stitches out and I felt okay, almost like nothing had happened. Dad came alone to pick us up. Caitlin and Joe were in school and Paul had returned to Omaha to Creighton where he was in school. Dad drove slowly (on another and better day he used to say, "50 miles per hour is enough for anybody"), now in a different car, a yellow Plymouth, and we were soon back to the farm house, Mom in bed resting, me sleeping on the couch downstairs in the living room.

That was the first time I ever had been touched by someone dying, and someone in my family. I'll never forget it. Things began to be a little more real, and life would not be just fun and games. I'll also never forget the words, smiles and hugs from it seemed like everyone at church, and even some of the kids at school. Even ole Jimmy who slugged me after the class play came up and said, "Geez Mick I'm glad you're back and you're okay." It seemed like in no time things were back to normal, school, the school bus, and playing in the yard and barn at home.

But I still remembered Grandma. She was a kind old lady and would always give me a nickel when we went to town, me spending it on ice cream at the drug store or at Duckwalls Five and Dime. But I remember most her rubbing my hand at home, generally at prayer time at night, and how it was so soothing, and all seemed so well with the world. She was old, she dressed funny, and maybe smelled a bit old, but I never loved anyone more.

It was one of those times with the shiny nickel that I had a real scare and got myself into a pickle. I must have been maybe six or seven years old. Grandma had given me that nickel and I was licking my ice cream cone. We were in Duckwalls Five and Dime. Somehow, I got separated from Mom and Grandma, looked for them all over the store, on the sidewalk out front, and no one in sight. I must have panicked and can't tell you why I did what I did. I began walking, first around the corner to Buckeye, and then that long walk all the way up to 14th street and the highway out of town. I walked east on it to the edge of the city limits and knocked on the door of this old couple living in a tiny, old house on Highway 40 and Brady (Dad must have known them from earlier days). I basically told them I was lost and couldn't find Mom or Dad. I guess they telephoned the farm phone, Mom answered and soon came up to get me. I don't remember a scolding. Hard to imagine how it all happened.

7

JOE'S SCRAPES – THE GRANARY

But Joe had his scrapes too.

Joe would deign to play with me, a lot more to be sure when I was maybe 9 or 10; by the time Joe went to Jr. High and High School, he considered me "too young" and "just a little kid." But before that, along with that failed boxing lesson he would let me hang out some. We would play catch with the baseball in summer, and toss the football in the Fall, and we did build snowmen when a big snow came once in a great while, maybe just a time or two. One of those play times was when we were playing up inside the old granary out by the silo. The idea was to climb up an old rickety ladder in the back of the granary and then "tight rope walk" the beams high up above. In spite of the fact there was some interesting stuff stored up there, including an old wooden sled with runners that had gathered dust as long as I could remember, I was afraid to climb the wooden slats of the ladder, partly because the steps were so far apart, partly because I would really get nervous when I saw Joe walking and almost skipping along the beams.

This time Joe beat me to the ladder, he could outrun me easy. He said, "Don't you come up, there's not enough room for the two of us. And besides, you're a scaredy-cat anyway." I yelled, "The hell I am. I've just got a lot more sense. I'm as good as you are." Paying no attention, he scrambled up the ladder and before I knew it was stepping on the beams from the back toward the front of the granary. But then it happened. I don't know if he tripped or what. Crrrrack! One of the old cross beams broke and down it came in pieces, Joe with it, to the hard ground floor of the granary. Joe was screaming in pain and yelled, "Go get Dad or Mom. I've got a damned nail through my hand and it's attached to a big board."

I ran for the house but stopped when I saw Dad running toward me from the hog house where he must have been working and heard the screams. And Mom ran out of the house, a worried look on her face. We all got back to the granary about the same time with Joe sitting on the ground, crying, and this really nasty nail going in one side of the palm of his hand and out the other. There was quite a lot of blood, maybe blood and tears. For some crazy reason I started laughing and got a hard slap on my butt by Dad. "Well, it is funny; look at that nail and the board." Mom still had a dish towel in her hand and Dad wrapped it around the hand and said, "Let's get to the car and get him to the hospital." I went along in the back seat of the old Plymouth. Dad pretty well tore down the farm lane, not saying much yet. Lucky we lived so close to town.

He drove up to the Emergency Room entrance, Mom opened the door, and immediately one of the nurses saw the situation, carefully put Joe in wheelchair, maneuvering him with the hand and board on his lap, and wheeled him inside. I was told to go to the waiting room, sit still and they'd call me when Joe was fixed up. I guess they must have given him a sedative or a big shot for the pain or maybe to deaden the place where the nail was, but when I was called into the hospital room, Joe was sitting up in bed, red eyed and with white gauze and bandage around his hand. For some odd reason, the board with the nail still in it was lying on a table beside the bed.

It wasn't long before they said he could go home, but just to be careful and keep the hand bandaged for a few days. Joe was a bit sheepish about it and not saying much. I just remember Dad saying, "I don't want to see either of you up there again. I'm sorry Joe, and I know it hurts, but you could have fallen on your head and things would be a lot worse." Joe said, "Yes sir," and looked over at me and whispered, "You're still a scaredy-cat." Mom said from the front seat, "Enough of that, especially from you scallywag, Joe. Don't give your little brother ideas."

I don't know when exactly, but probably sometime after Joe had flown the coop from the farm to work in town or at the State 4-H camp, I did climb up above on the same old beams. But carefully, and the fun and thrill of it was gone. I never did get over that memory of Joe crying and in pain on that hard ole' ground. And I forgave him for not wanting to play with me.

8

COMING OF AGE AND SPORTS

Aside from Joe, I had plenty of time to play games with buddies or alone on the farm, but about this time, now in 6th grade at Garfield School, life had a big change – competitive sports! Not only did I go out for the grade school basketball team but actually made the squad, maybe on the second five. I experienced my first male teacher, Mr. Robson. What's in a child's memories? He seemed handsome, with a good head of blond hair, wore a suit and tie to school, but most of all, was my first "teacher-jock." He would become the grade school basketball coach, and I guess, a role model for all us guys. Life now would begin to revolve around sports and my first team experiences, namely basketball and then baseball in the spring on the school playground.

We practiced in the Garfield gymnasium. It must have been a half-size court, but it seemed like Madison Square Garden to me. Memories are sparse, but I do know that I played regularly in practice, was a guard responsible for bringing the ball up court. My budding mediocrity in sports was in evidence, but I was no klutz or slouch either. There was no lack of motivation. Our basketball heroes were from Kansas State and K.U. There is more to tell, much more, but I don't know where in my story. But K-State had Dick Knostman, K.U. had Clyde Lovellete and then B. H. Born and then no less than Wilt Chamberlain. Many a night in junior high and high school were marked by my listening to K-State games at the side of the old radio in the family room and scoring with Xs and Os. Good friend Luke Zimmerman was the true athlete, even back then in grade school, the "natural" who was a high scorer and could make those pretty outside shots. I would throw one in just once in a while. I can remember Loren Beasley, also a natural, playing the forward or center slot.

I can recall only one game, against that powerhouse of Talmage Grade School. For perspective, Talmage is a spot in the road along a paved county road some eight miles north of town, but they had a tall center who would later become a friend in high school, Clay Wommer. This was my first experience at actually having a uniform for sports! I can't recall the colors, but the jersey and baggy shorts on my, guessing, skinny 70 lb. frame, must have been a sight to see. But we all felt like K-State or K.U. stars in those uniforms. I don't know how that game with Talmage came out, but a momentous day for me, Mick the substitute, was to come.

On the playground, recess was still the most important activity other than sports after school; there were lots of races run, and once again, I turned out to be one slow farm boy. There were girls who could beat me and other slowpokes; this brings first mention of Kayla Scott, a regular gazelle, one of the class cuties who later would shine as cheer leader, star on the stage in junior high and high school plays, and strangely enough, one of the few girls I never dated (but brother Joe did have a thing for her older sister in those years). I digress. Her father was an executive, I think, for the only real corporation in Abilene in those days, the Five and Dime Duckwall Stores.

A big activity in those days on the playground in the 1940s was tether ball, a vigorous competition of two, each trying to bat a soccer ball on a rope around a pole before the other person could wrap it around before you. Kids with creative Dads (and not busy farmers) cajoled ole' Dad to put one up for them at home. My Dad did not do this, but on the other hand, I would have in junior high and high school the best basketball court ever in the hayloft of our big old hay barn.

A great institution at Garfield Grade School was the end of year picnic. We had an outing to the nearby high school athletic field for baseball or such, and then a sack, picnic lunch. My all-time favorite in those days was cold fried chicken, bread and butter sandwiches, maybe an apple, and probably cookies or candy bar for dessert. The picnic also seemed to usher in the warm and even hot weather. There was no air conditioning in the school, so those hot spring and fall days meant for lethargy in the classroom.

An interesting phenomenon of growing up: the anticipation and envy of growing up, but short-term, of wanting to grow and get to that next level - Junior High and then High School! Immediately next door to Garfield was Abilene Jr. High, formerly Abilene High School. We witnessed the "big" kids each day next door playing baseball or hanging out in front of the school before classes. It seemed much "cooler" than our lives. There is a famous picture in the annals of Abilene, one Dwight D. Eisenhower in baseball uniform for the Abilene High School Cowboys, taken in front of the same building I describe.

Next sports memories will come in Junior High, I will tell more on that later when I grow to age 12 and move on over to the Junior High, puberty and new times. But there's a tale or two yet from Garfield. Namely, there were evening activities throughout the year, all held once again in the school auditorium-gym. At what I recall as the school carnival, I ate too many hot dogs and threw up on that nice hardwood floor of the gymnasium; it was months or years before I could eat the dogs again. Vomiting thereafter would come only upon severe illness or a couple of beer busts in high school. I think they boiled the frankfurters in a big pot; that must have been it.

Did I talk of the grade school days when I sat in the back of the classroom doing these fantastic drawings, probably during penmanship class? I would do panoramic Korean War Scenes with aerial dogfights between US Thunder Jets or Saber Jets and Russian Migs, the skies full of action. Another topic was Indian wars but based on a movie I saw in those days - either Hurons or Iroquois with the strip of hair in the middle of a shaved head, but with bows and arrows, tomahawks, knives, and pants and shirts with the buckskin fringe on the leggings. But the masterpieces would come with immensely complex drawings of Road Runner cartoons featuring all the gadgets that Wiley Coyote would get from ACME company to try to thwart the roadrunner. With some training I might have made something of that, but alas and alas. Oh, we had races to finish the assignment each day in penmanship class, the main result my lousy, lousy handwriting.

A moment of hilarity from the same days was the grade school lunchroom scene. Many of us brought sack lunches which in my case would mean a sandwich, perhaps some sliced carrots, some chips, an apple and some cookies. One little fellow delighted in taking a banana and slowly squashing it in his hands until it was a pulpy mess, and then slowly eating it. We howled with laughter. But most memorable was Ricky Howland and his lunch. Ricky probably weighed in at 250 pounds, even in grade school. His lunch consisted in a package of lunch meat directly from the market, you know, in white wrapping paper with a string around it; then a loaf of bread, an entire package of cookies, and perhaps a bunch of bananas. It all soon disappeared before our eyes. There were moments of hilarious, stomach hurting laughter.

Back to the sports. In 7th and 8th grade I played JHS football and probably weighed less than 100 pounds, and of course I wanted to play center, since that was what brother Joe played for the high school. He indeed was my role model in those days. We practiced on the old athletic field north of the Abilene High School field and stadium. I recall we suited up in the junior high building and then walked or ran to the practice field. Funny, but one of the memories is lining up opposite Rip Warner, a big, big boy who would have great days ahead at AHS. I think Rip took it a bit easy on me in those practices. I believe Luke Zimmerman was the quarterback, Loren Beasley the half back, and then the rest of us were the grunts. I remember those guys who were friends of mine and about the same athletic ability, I would have them out to the farm to play, all of us "stalwart athletes." I'm sure I've left a bunch of hardnosed guys out.

The Junior High showed its age. It was a red brick building but with hard wood floors, lots of stairways up and down, all very creaky. Just fleeting images were my math teacher Mr. Morganson's home room, the big room where we had "shop," the big airy study hall with large windows facing the playground and ball field, and the classroom of Mrs. Howard, the fine English teacher and director of drama. I also recall Mr. Albegard of science class. My memory of "science" was when he stirred a glass of ice water, showed the condensation, and there was some lesson to be learned, somehow, out of that. Apparently not much stuck with me.

Like the rooms of the farmhouse, the rooms of Abilene Junior High all had memories for me.

Shop class was obligatory, and we were expected to do projects. I somehow managed to make a lamp and an end table, both out of walnut. But I think future engineer and computer geek Ralph Book must have helped me with the wiring; my less than rudimentary knowledge of electricity dates back to those days. But shop was full of fun, lots of laughing, and the telling of dirty jokes. A curious memory comes to mind: the day the Polish immigrant boy arrived, and we became somewhat aware that there were serious events going on outside of Abilene. It must have been 1953 or so. I think the immigrant family, Catholic of course, became tenant farmers east of our farm in Abilene.

Much of the time spent in shop class was spent heehawing when someone farted, the louder and the smellier, the greater our reaction. And too much carrying on or fooling around brought punishment - swats from the wooden board the teacher wielded so well, probably ironically made out of high-grade walnut as well. I don't know if I got more than one or two, but the "regulars," Ray Solter comes to mind, wore out that board.

Recess was big for us. There were games, but all according to season. We played tag football; you carried a strip of cloth in your rear pocket and were "tackled" when someone could grab it out of the pocket. The idea being: no roughness or tackling. Baseball was a great favorite, softball that is, a pretty democratic game because we played "work up," and everyone had a crack at each position and a chance to bat. Ole Mick was just "average," but the big boys, good athletes that is, spent a lot of time intentionally hitting the ball in foul territory and breaking windows in the study hall. Luke Zimmerman and Ray Solter were the ones I recall most. I do not know where it all happened, but much of the time, or spare time, was spent telling dirty jokes, our "sex education" in Abilene.

It was in the study hall with the broken windows that I associated the coming of puberty, the interest in girls and in particular ogling the well-endowed girls. In effect big boobs! I won't mention names, but you know who you are! A tight white blouse or better yet, a cotton or woolen sweater brought moments of happiness to us all. As for studying, I suppose some work got done, but that's not what I remember. An aside: I did not begin to take academics seriously until about sophomore year in high school, more on that later. But I think native "smarts" kept me somewhat in the game without working too hard at it in Jr. High.

An important memory was drama class, an extra-curricular activity in those days, with Mrs. Howard. We did plays in both 7th and 8th grades, and I was fairly good at it. I can remember one play "Auggie Evans Private Eye" by title only. I can't remember a thing about the play, but I think I had the lead and was able to be around several of the pretty young things in 8th grade.

A related activity was to memorize "readings" and declaim them at contests like the declamation contest in Enterprise, a nearby town. One time I did a "shtick" as a sports announcer with several props: a microphone, a Walter Cronkite hat and maybe a pipe. The reading won a blue ribbon that day.

In those same days, perhaps now junior high or even high school, there were the cokes, etc. and the flirting at the Malt Shop, a semi-sleazy place on 3rd street, or at Cunningham's' drug store with the big kids, with the pin ball machines and sneaking looks at the girly magazines back in the corner, but also checking the latest football and baseball stories. I managed to get a couple of quarters together to get a few of those sports magazines, particularly anything about the New York Yankees and Mickey Mantle.

More sports in Junior High. Football I already talked about a little. The uniforms were funny, the helmets funnier yet; there was a hierarchy, the 7th graders getting the old-fashioned ones we can maybe associate now with Bronco Nagurski in 1919! The 8th graders wore "modern" helmets which we seventh graders would eventually inherit the following year. I remember bus trips to our two or three games, once to Concordia, Kansas, some 30-40 miles away, once to Hillsboro, Kansas to the South. We played in the afternoon before I imagine whatever students got out of class to see the game and a few adults – players' parents. I have a picture that says our record was 2-1. Oh, the main activity on the bus ride to and from the game was all of us singing "99 bottles of beer on the wall," up to 99 and back down again. I surmise the bus driver and the coach needed a beer or two when they got home that night.

Basketball for me was a much bigger deal. As usual with my "average" only abilities, I would just barely make the squad, I think maybe 9th or 10th on a 10 man squad.

Practices were held at the "old" high school, still in operation then, and at times in an old venerable place in Abilene, the old "city building," a drafty small gym just north of the city library. I'll get back to games later, but there is just one memory associated with that place which I need to recount. Back in grade school in the city basketball tournament, Garfield played McKinley school for the title, 6th grade it was (all our grade schools were named for assassinated presidents!). I was allowed in the game in the final minutes, a token substitution I think, and proceeded to ever so lightly tap the fingers of the crack McKinley guard, my introduction to R.M. Woodston, this while trying to guard him in a final desperation shot. Garfield must have had the lead at the time. Anyway, R.M. proceeded to make both foul shots and win the game for them. Among two or three low moments of my Abilene sports career, this was perhaps the lowest. Wracked with crying after the game, that's how I remember it. What I cannot remember however, is even one word of condemnation by teammates. I think there was much slapping on the shoulder and "That's all right, you did your best" sort of repartee. It is a lesson of life learned only years later – maybe we are our own worst enemy when it comes to punishing ourselves.

But there were greater, really happy moments associated with the old city auditorium gym. In those years even the high school varsity games were held in the auditorium. I think mainly on Friday nights. But I doubt I ever missed a game. We would actually sit on the "stage," with the regular audience facing us in the shape of a inverted "U." Memories are fading, but there was a terrific black athlete who played center, a sharp shooting guard who dated my sister Caitlin a bit in those years, and the excitement of it all. All this was prior to 1955, a watershed year for lots of reasons I'll get into later, when I was a freshman at AHS and we moved to the shiny, sparkling "field house" in the new high school. The new gym had one major change—the new court has glass backboards! This was progress and a quantum leap in our lives as athletes!

That old drafty county gym brought a wonderful memory of growing up in Abilene. The county tournament in basketball. The games were held at the downtown old city building. Teams were from local Abilene schools, but also all the tiny consolidated schools in the county plus other small county towns. It was a full two days I think, and you might be seeing Rural Consolidated school playing Woodbine or Enterprise. There were lots of country boys in those old-style basketball shorts and jerseys. We all spent many hours watching, probably swilling down cokes and eating hot dogs and assorted junk.

Just one more memory from those days and basketball. 4-H Basketball. The Abilene Aggies, my team, was playing a game out at Rural Center, a consolidated school about 10 miles south of Abilene. The memory was that Joe my brother was still around, and we actually played on the same team. And yours truly got hot for once in his life and made several long baskets. Only time in my life.

And not far from that country basketball court for 4-H was the public golf course with sand greens south of town. My buddies and I went through a phase and maybe went three or four times, playing in the dry pasture, putting on the sand greens and dodging cow pies. It was cheap, no one complained; there was no talk or envy of the country club set, but I did remember driving by the country club on the Highway 40 By Pass and seeing all that water shooting up in the air for their irrigation.

9

JOE AS MODEL, FOOTBALL AND THE CONCUSSION

As mad as I would get at Joe for not letting me play with him on the farm, those times were not many and tended to fade away with time. Much more often, I really had him as sort of a hero, and he became a role-model for me, I'm thinking from maybe 7th or 8th grade and high school years. He was four years older than me so by high school in 1956-1959 he was off at college up at Marquette University in faraway Milwaukee with a naval ROTC scholarship, but consciously or not, Joe was still with me.

I was a skinny runt the whole time growing up. It didn't have anything to do with my appetite because I never missed a meal, but it was related to Joe. He was a lot stockier than me; about six-foot-tall and maybe 160 pounds, heavy enough in those days now the early 1950s, to play high school football and even make the first team. Joe played in the line, center sometimes, and guard the other. So when I started playing football in Jr. High, I wanted to be just like him. I guess the coaches wanted every boy to have a chance to participate or else they were really hard up because I played center in 8th grade, and guard freshman year. If you can believe it, at I think 114 pounds.

I asked for and got Joe's high school number, 32. Different than Joe, some of my scrapes or problems did not come on the farm, although there were a few, but more at school or like that car wreck I already told about. In this case we were practicing football on the ole' Abilene High School athletic field in front of the old wooden stands. It must have been a scrimmage because we were running plays. I don't remember a thing except waking up in the hospital in what seemed an all-white room, white walls, ceiling, even bed and bed sheets. Mom, Dad, and a couple of football buddies were in the room, remembering mainly Larry, the pudgy lineman. I felt just fine but did not know what had happened or remember anything. It was Larry who came up to the side of the bed, a worried look on his face and saying, "Mick are you all right? What a scare!"

I said, "Larry, I don't remember a thing. What happened?" He began to laugh, and then apologized, saying, "Geez I'm sorry but it was so funny. We're lining up for a play and you are in the center position getting ready to hike the ball. I come up and say, 'Hey Mick, I'm playing center. What the hell are you doing? Get out of the way.'" I said, "What do you mean. Of course, I'm playing center; ain't that what I'm supposed to be doing?"

In those days I guess I had what we used to call "getting your bell rung." Later that evening in the hospital room, ole' Doc Bernard came in, smiled, put his hand on my arm, and said, "Mick, you sure picked a funny way to get out of football practice. You've had a concussion, but you've coming out of it fine and I think you'll be fit as a fiddle tomorrow morning. We're going to keep you here over night just to make sure. But there'll be no practice for you for a few days."

After I guess a couple of weeks, I was back at it, suited up for football practice. We were in a scrimmage, me back to playing guard, and ran a play. Suddenly I got a splitting headache and walked over to the sideline and told the coaches about it. All agreed it was time for Mick O'Brien to stop playing football. I don't recall being upset at all, but I guess mainly relieved. I still had freshman basketball and track in the spring. But it turned out to be a stroke of good luck. The next year, now I'm a sophomore, I did speech class and was invited to join the Debate team. That really turned out well.

10

THE END OF THE LANE, THE BUS AND WINTERTIME

In all those years from first school days to maybe junior high we kids rode the country school bus this after Paul was gone and working. Joe, Caitlin, and I, the baby of the family, would troop down the lane early in the morning to catch our yellow bus. We did it every day for so many years. But I recall that often it was very cold and uncomfortable. And you would be bundled up in sweaters, heavy coat, stocking caps, gloves, and galoshes.

We used to play a game while waiting, "Scissor Steps" or "Mama May I" I think it was called, the idea being that each person had to follow the leader in whatever kind of steps the other took. All this took place on the asphalt pavement. I can't even remember the object of the game other than imitating giant steps, scissor steps, etc., but it was great fun. It made the time pass. It had the added attraction of building suspense doing it while cars were slowly coming toward you from the distance. We cut it close sometimes.

Because we lived close to town, really only one mile from the east city limit, and because the bus changed its route and direction each six weeks, for six weeks we would be last on in the morning and first off at night; first on and last off the next six weeks. I can't recall exactly how it went, but the idea was that one time we got on the bus and rode for nearly an hour and a half before getting to school, the same getting off the next six weeks. It probably would have been more efficient and better for all of us to walk the mile to the city limits and another mile and a half to school, but I guess we were too small. In later years I did enjoy walking or riding my bike to school in Abilene.

There was always lots of shouting and talking on the bus and a few pranks. Mr. Holt or "Hootie" - our drivers - must have been tolerant people. I can remember one time when some of the older guys started a fire in the back seats. But more often I remember the long rides, reading books or just staring out into space. A treat would be to see a coyote or pheasant, but that was rare. But on the trip home after school, it was a joyous moment to bound off the bus and start the walk up the lane to see a smiling Mom who always had a treat or snack for me when I got into the house, especially cookies or cake.

It was then that the outside games would come, basketball in the barn, baseball with the lath stick and then the afternoon radio programs. And the chores were in there some place because there was no way to get out of them. After that, finally, came suppertime with the six o'clock news on the radio.

A last note about the bus days. One morning while waiting for the bus and playing games, my sister Caitlin left her books and violin (in its case) on the ground near the highway. A neighbor drove in the lane that day and smashed the violin to smithereens! Caitlin burst into tears, and Joe and I kind of just stood by, nothing we could really do. I'm not sure exactly why, whether for lack of money, or Caitlin's sadness, that violin was never replaced, and Caitlin moved on to other interests in Junior High and High School. That would have been maybe 1950 to 1954.

There was a whole other memory about the end of the lane and old Highway 40. It had to do with weather. Just once or twice in those years, we would have what they in Kansas called a blizzard, heavy snow and winds. The highway would be frozen over with several inches of ice and snow, all traffic stopped. There would be a couple of semi-trucks jackknifed, and various cars and pickups stopped. We would put on every stitch of winter clothes we had and go down to look at it. Just like Dad in Nebraska, the fence row in the field next to the highway would be obliterated – you walked over the top. We weren't there long – too cold.

A different memory was when the ice and snow would melt; it was the only time we had water running in the ditch next to the road. I would have friends from school come out and we would tromp around in the water and made small wooden boats to "sail" along it. Great fun. But maybe just once or twice like I said over the years.

Worse, for Mom and Dad at least, was the incredible muddy farm lane up to the house, almost impassable. You figured out a way to maneuver through, around and on top of the ruts. Dad did not have enough money to put down new gravel every year, although he did once in a while. More than once we took the Ford tractor down the lane, with a big logging chain on the back, to pull out people who would either drive too fast or not know how to maneuver it and get stuck. I only had the problem once, way up outside of town north when I was catting around with brother Joe's '51 Chevy, paying more attention to the sound of the pipes than the mud. To make it worse, it was the father of one of my girl friends who had to pull me out.

11

CHORES, ELFRED AND THE 12 GUAGE, THE ROCK ISLAND LINE

When I was young, maybe 9 or 10, I was pretty unaware of everything going on. But as I grew a bit older, now maybe twelve or thirteen, maybe in sixth or seventh grade, it seemed that life was bigger, more complicated, more fun, but full of stuff I want to tell about. There was more work on the farm, and I began to have an inkling of what was going on around me. So much was going on, yet nothing was changing. By now I was too big to sit on Dad's lap (or Mom's for that matter) but I was big enough to start to help out on the farm. Joe was around early on, but not much later first of all due to his attacks of hay fever from trying to work in the field; he found a job at the General Store in town. Caitlin worked on Saturday's as a clerk at the J.C. Penney's store. Before town though Joe and I probably spent more time together, not necessarily having fun, than any time after. We would toss the football around in the yard, but he complained, "You're no fun; I can throw long ones to you, but you can't throw it back. Let's go in."

There was no lack of work to do on the farm as a boy; Dad could always find chores for us to do. When less than ten years of age, I can recall one of my jobs was to take the trash out to a barrel north of the house and burn it. When enough non-burnable stuff had accumulated, we hauled the whole kit and kaboodle up to the pasture to a spot we called the "dump," on a hill on the north 80 acres. From there you had a marvelous view of the whole Smokey Hill River Valley below, the town of Abilene to the southwest. There was lots of brush, old wire, pop bottles, cans and plain junk at the dump, a perfect spot for cottontail rabbits to hide, so when we went rabbit hunting, that was always a mandatory stop along the route. One of us kids would jump on the top to scare out the rabbits and the farm dog would chase them down.

It was about this time, maybe I was ten or eleven and we were visiting relatives of Dad's up near Talmage. My cousin Elfred was a real "good ole' boy" country kid about ten years older than I. He wore overalls and had those old round granny glasses for his near-sighted eyes. He chewed tobacco (and that made him a "big man"), had a crooked grin through his yellowed teeth, but knew his way around local fishing for catfish and hunting all kinds of small animals like rabbits, coyotes, and even taking pot shots at the prairie dogs. He had promised to take Joe and me out to do some real hunting with a 12-gauge shotgun, and this was the day. He said the good hunting was along Talmage Crick, but the only way to get there was to go in his old beat up jeep over the railroad tracks and a railroad bridge. It was an old army surplus jeep and did not instill confidence in me. I said, "What about the trains? This is the old Rock Island Line." He smiled that crooked smile and said, "Shit, they only come twice a day, early in the morning and one at night. You a 'fraidy cat or something?" My teeth were rattled as we drove over the ties, over the small trestle and he pulled off on the other side and we walked down to the crick. We must have walked for thirty minutes up and down, and nothing turned up, but he said, "No sense wasting all this. Mick, you want to learn to shoot a shotgun?" I was scared out of my pants, but said, "Sure."

"Here." He handed me the big gun about as tall as me, I was just ten remember. He said, "Hold it firm, the stock up against your cheek, take aim and pull the trigger nice and slow." I still don't know if this was a big joke for the bastard. So I took aim at a stump, the gun tight against my cheek, pulled the trigger and "Blam," the kick knocking me to the ground.

Elfred and Joe were laughing their asses off as I sat on the ground, rubbing my cheek. "Must not 'a held it tight enough," Elfred heehawed after spitting up a big glob of "Red Man." "Get up, not much else going on here, we got to get back."

We walked back up the creek, up the bank and to the old jeep. Elfred started it up and pulled back on to the tracks. Just as we were about half way across the trestle, I heard the piercing sound of the whistle of that Rock Island steam engine, and that mother was right behind us. "Oh shit," Elfred said, gunned the engine, damned near tossing us all out of the jeep into the crick, but managed to just clear the trestle, yanked the steering wheel and jerked us off the track, almost turning us over in the process. "I reckon that was just one of those unscheduled freights heading down to Abilene." End of story; that was the last time I would ever go hunting with that cousin. And to boot the next morning the whole side of my face was black and blue and still hurt. Joe smirked at it all, but he got his come 'uppins the next summer when we were baling hay and good ole' Elfred gave him a chew of "Red Man" and Joe threw up in the bathroom of the farmhouse at dinner time. I still wonder what would have happened if that old clunker of a jeep would have stalled on the tracks. And, oh yeah, that was the last time I ever picked up a 12-guage. Not so funny.

There was a fun school memory about that time. I must have been just 10 or so because Joe and Caitlin were still in school. I don't know how Mom and Dad could afford it, but once a week they gave us "lunch money," I'm thinking 35 or 50 cents to eat lunch downtown. Joe and Caitlin would meet me at Duckwalls, the Five and Dime. It had a lunch counter, and we would all get the same thing: a toasted cheese sandwich, mashed potatoes and gravy, a pickle and maybe a small coke or root beer. Nothing could have tasted better to me, and the best part, there was a nickel or dime left to buy a five-cent pack of bubble gum and baseball cards and maybe a root beer barrel or two. I could spend a good 30 minutes browsing my way through their toy section and on over to the Roy Rogers or Gene Autry toy guns and holsters and Red Ryder B-B guns. Joe and

Caitlin would have gone on, but it was a straight walk of maybe six or seven blocks up to Garfield School and back for the afternoon classes and maybe sports.

About that time I went out for basketball on the grade school team, now maybe in 6th grade, and made the team, maybe as a substitute.

12

FOOD, BUTCHERING, THE AX, THE CHICKEN HEAD, THE GARDEN

I want to tell about the chores on the farm, but I guess that's related a lot to our food. So I'll talk about it first.

The farm was not totally self-sufficient in food but was not far from it. Meat came from the chickens we raised, tiny from the hatchery, pork and beef butchered on the farm in the open driveway of the granary, later to be packaged and frozen in the old locker plant located on the south side of the Union Pacific tracks in old Abilene. There were lots of vegetables in season from a large, one-acre garden immediately to the northeast of the farmhouse, and many of these were canned for winter usage. Fruit had to be purchased in the local grocery stores and was seasonal, but it also was canned.

We had eggs from the chickens and dairy products from the one or two milk cows (milk, butter, cream) Dad kept around most of the time. We had homemade ice cream once in a while in the summertime, but most desserts were baked goods: pies, cakes, cookies, and homemade bread, much of it out of Mom's oven. In spite of being a wheat farmer, Dad always purchased flour in town in five or ten-pound bags, just like most farmers in the region. Spices, coffee, and sugar were all bought in town. I recall that shopping or "trading" as Dad liked to call it, was done generally on Saturdays and almost always, in part, paid with store money at the RHV Store ("Real Honest Value") in exchange for eggs and cream brought in each week by Dad. I am fairly sure my brother Joe worked for some time at the store during high school years; sister Caitlin worked at J.C. Penney's which still had the overhead cable system for sending receipts, change etc. to cashiers sitting upstairs in the office as well as the old-style tin ceiling. I probably worked more on the farm than any of my brothers or sister due to one reason or another, but more on that later.

I remember the RHV store, a type of general store in its time. There was the feed part out back with high stacks of 50 and 100 pound sacks of grain and feed for all animals, the creamery part with scales, etc. Inside, the appliances, the long hardware part, but my favorite was the sports section where I would ogle the new leather baseball gloves that smelled so good and had names like Stan Musial, Mickey Mantle, Ted Williams or Allie Reynolds on them, and the real Louisville Sluggers autographed by the same heroes. The RHV also had a shoe store across the street, a clothing store and a grocery. We bought shoes there, but groceries were at the old A & P, famous then for its low profit margin; I guess that's why they went out of business, and Zoll's food store on the south side, close to the old creamery and the locker plant where we kept frozen meat from butchering on the farm, and besides, they were Catholics.

Back to food and how we got it. Butcher day was a big event, almost always in cold weather as I recall (I guess to help with keeping the meat cool, fewer flies or insects, etc. It brings to mind the day we had to butcher a steer that bloated in the alfalfa field east of the farmhouse.) The hog or steer was killed by a blow to the head with a hammer or perhaps a bullet to the brain, was strung up on a pulley attached to the scaffolding of the granary, in the driveway, the blood drained, and Dad and his helper(s) would butcher, trim the hide and fat away and make the big cuts. I don't know where Dad learned all that, I guess by helping others and doing. It seemed like I was always too young, too immature or just plain disinterested to learn much. The whole experience of growing up on the farm was a mainly pleasant one and obviously a good memory, that's why I'm writing this book, but I am amazed at how little I learned that stuck with me, at least in practical skills. I can recall getting close to being nauseated with I had to stand around and help Dad with a mechanical task, as a "gofer" or whatever. I guess I had the strong genes in other areas like music, languages, history, and book-learning.

I can remember one cold, icy day when you could see your breath in the cold air, butchering day for a steer. I stood by watching when all of a sudden Dad handed me this steamy, warm object, saying, "Here. Hold this". I can't describe the sensation; I didn't feel like fainting, but I guess the word is squeamish (I should have known then that I would never have an aptitude for medical school). It was the liver, a large hunk of mass, a pleasantly warm, pliable, mysterious piece of flesh. I have never been particularly fond of that organ since.

Other things I remember of butchering day were the final product, the nicely packaged meat in the cold storage locker in old Abilene near the railroad tracks. I can recall innumerable times accompanying Mom or Dad into that frozen room to our locker to pick out meat to take home for meals. I always had a real fear the freezer door would close, and we would not able to get out, even though there was a large knob contraption to open the door from the inside.

Another memory, this when butchering a pig or hog, was that of the fresh pork tenderloin that I enjoyed more than any other cut of meat. I also liked the thick bacon with real flavor which we always had for breakfast. Related, but unrelated: there is a single memory of high school days much later when we went over to Solomon, Kansas, to drink beer in the tavern; one night they served "mountain oysters" in the bar; served with ice cold beer. There were days on the farm designated as "castration" days - I can remember watching but not doing, a good thing. In those days the tenderloin tasted to me like the finest cut of beef steak. Charcoal cookers and outside barbecues were unheard of; all meat was fried on the kitchen stove or boiled, broiled or baked in the oven. I cannot recall eating much beef steak growing up, in spite of raising and butchering the beef. We ate lots of roasts, hamburger (us kids liked it) and only an occasional fried steak, usually overdone.

I am sure we ate far more chicken than beef or pork. We killed the chickens by cutting off their heads with an ax, later dunking the rest of the chicken in boiling water to take off the feathers, cleaning out the insides, cutting up and frying. Dad would do the honors with the ax. I can remember like yesterday the big shade tree by the chicken house, the big stump under that tree with two nails; the chicken head was supposed to fit between, the ax planted in the middle awaiting the task. Dad would catch the squawking victim for that Sunday with a long "chicken hook", an affair with a round wooden handle, a long, semi-flexible steel rod with a curved hook on the end, much like the curve of the old shepherd's staff. Often I was sent with the hook to catch the chicken and bring it squawking to Dad. Our Border Collie "Lady," a black and white sheepdog, loved this part and always seemed to know when the fatal moment would be, barking close by in excited anticipation. Between the squawking of the chicken and the barking of the dog, it was a lively scene. Dad with one swift blow would part the head from the body and sling the body away. That's when the show started. The decapitated bird would bounce, stumble, jump and bound for what seemed an eternity, the dog jumping and barking nearby, until the body of the chicken finally fell motionless to the ground. I've heard tell and have seen those farmers who put the chicken under their arm, grab the head and neck, and pop it, instantly (I surmise) killing the chicken. For some reason we never used that method.

My time came. "Mick, go get us a chicken for supper". The problem was I could never seem to accomplish the swift killing with one blow of the ax. It was either a series of blows, some of them striking the chicken in the middle of the head or missing all together. I can recall a time or two of a leaping chicken, head half on, half off, me chasing it trying to give it the "coup de grace." That was just one of my adventures with the chickens while growing up. It's amazing I still love to eat them.

Mom did the plucking of the chicken feathers in big pans outside the house (for obvious reasons), although there were times when all of us plucked as well, I guess when we had sold several fryers to town people, another small source of farm income. If it was cold at all you see the steam coming from the boiling water in the crisp, icy air. It there was any dietary staple in the family, it was chicken, fried in the warm months, and baked with wonderful dressing, like a Thanksgiving turkey, especially on Sunday in the Fall and Winter. Both remain favorites in spite of literally hundreds of such meals growing up. At any rate I was a klutz with the ax, but hey, I did it right once in a while.

Garden Day was an annual and important event. Hopefully after the last frost (and you never knew for sure when that would be), it was a family enterprise of sorts, that is, when any of the kids could be rounded up to help. Paul at this point in his life helped little, was more like a boarder with his job in the business world. Joe and Caitlin helped for sure when they were younger. There's got to be a lot I am not old enough to remember, but by the time I do remember they were often gone on many weekend activities from school or were working in town.

It was always on a Saturday. Dad would plow the entire area with our little Ford tractor, approximately an acre immediately east and northeast of the farmhouse. Then rows would be set for beans, onions, radishes and the like. Dad said, "Mick, you hoe the rows for me. And try to make them straight." "Fat chance," I thought. A very large area was set aside for potatoes; I can recall watching Dad or Mom cut up the seed potatoes, always with an "eye" in each bit, and planting. (I also helped dig potatoes, small ones were eaten with sweet peas for a delicious part of dinner in late summer if I'm not mistaken; and the big potatoes were dug during the fall, often with the field muddy with fall rains, to be stored in the cool and damp basement of the house.) I would do a lot of the hoeing, making the rows, planting seeds or onion sets or the like.

We had an annual strawberry patch grown in the shade of big elm trees near the house and had wonderful strawberries in season. (I don't know if it's any coincidence they were near the septic tank.) I loved them mashed up on vanilla ice cream or on angel food cake. But I could never eat them like my parents: in a bowl with rich farm cream. Strawberry jam, jelly and preserves however became a lifelong favorite.

Like most kids I did not like many of the vegetables while growing up, but can remember delicious, fresh, tasty, "real" tomatoes. Ah, cucumbers and sliced onions with vinegar. There were lots of green beans, peas, carrots, and radishes. But I did not like beets, spinach, turnips, most of the stuff my parents really enjoyed. Mom would say, "Try them; they're good!" After a few times she gave up. But then there was the sweet corn! It was always planted in the far reaches of the garden, to be ready a bit ahead of the field corn grown in a large field on the farm well east of the garden. Mom and Dad always said the sweet corn was better, more tender and with more flavor, but I liked it all, able to devour three or four large ears at a sitting. I can recall being sent to the cornfield with a paper grocery bag, filling up the bag, shucking the husks and getting the ears ready for the boiling pot. My interest in biology and particularly (what is it called?) entomology started and ended there with the variety of bugs, worms, and caterpillars working the field corn. But this was deemed normal and doing little harm. You picked out the bugs, lopped off the bad part of the ear and got on with it. That fresh corn was one of the joys of my youth.

Canning took place throughout the summer when the vegetables were ready, another incredibly busy and hard-working day for my mother. We stored the mason jars in the cool basement. It became a matter of bringing up the empty jars, cobwebby and dusty, washing and sterilizing them, cooking the vegetables and doing the actual canning. Mom used paraffin to seal the lids. I recall lots of fruit canning - peaches, plums, apricots, cherries and the making of jams and preserves. Mom and Dad would bring home bushel baskets of a given fruit in season and do the canning. It was a day-long project, hard work most unappreciated by me at that time. I wonder now why they did all that and am sure it was a combination of factors. They loved the taste of those goodies in off season, in the middle of winter. It was also a custom, the way farm folks had been doing it for generations. However, I am sure the economic factor had to do with it also. It was probably cheaper to buy in quantity during season than buying canned goods that did not taste as good or were not as fresh. I recall they used a very large, heavy duty pressure cooker for a lot of the canning, and I grew up with the fear of that thing exploding, a fear I'm sure I got from talk of the actual thing happening. I have not got within striking distance of one since.

13

MORE CHORES, ASSORTED SHIT, MILKING AND LUKE ZIMMERMAN

Back to the chores. I also soon was in charge of gathering the eggs. We gathered two or three times a day; if you did not, the breakage would be up, and that meant lost money. I can recall those clucking Leghorns or Plymouth Rock hens pecking at me while I tried to maneuver a hand under their soft undersides and snatch away the eggs. Inevitably I would forget to do this chore, or put it off and play instead, so then there was a mess in the nests. The hens would peck open the eggs. You had to keep fresh straw baled from wheat stubble after harvest in the nests, so that too was a job. It meant cleaning out the old soiled straw and replacing it with new.

Later on, now perhaps 12 or 13 years of age, I was gradually given a whole series of outside chores, at first less in the morning because of school I guess, then both morning and night. I can recall most of that routine like it were today: feeding grain to the chickens, chicken mash or the like and making sure the water pans were full. Then moving on over to the silo where I would climb up in the silo and shovel ensilage down the chute and then on to a long feed bunk for the cattle. I spent many hours inside that silo when filling time came in the Summer, my job being to guide the filler or blower pipe with a long rope attached to it and get the silage spread evenly throughout the silo, then tramping it down. You had to wear goggles and a face mask to protect your eyes since it was very dirty. There was always talk of the danger of poisonous gases building up in the silo. They mixed a type of molasses with the ensilage and I can recall vividly the sweet smell when months later I would be inside pitching the now well-matured stuff down the chute to the cattle.

A digression on silo filling (with corn, sorghum or maybe milo). It was an exciting time for me and a bit dangerous I thought. Someone (I never did it) had to climb the silo, perhaps with a height equivalent to a six or seven story building, make his way around the top, let down a rope and attach it to a pulley to pull the blower pipe up to the top. I have always been afraid of heights, so that moment terrified me. One time, neighbor Grady Zimmerman scooted up the outside of the silo like a mountain goat, using the steel tie bars as grips and steps. I was sure he was going to fall. The normal way to do the task was to climb up the iron rung steps of the silo which were enclosed by an oval brick wall, then walk the edge of the top of the silo which had a steel railing and attach the pulley. Grady did it different.

There was only one bad time. I was inside with the goggles on guiding the blow pipe. I don't remember much other than feeling a big dizzy and then waking up with Dad right there. He said, "Got to get you out of here Mick and into the fresh air." He half carried me over to the stairs and said, "Are you okay to climb down? Take a few deep breaths before you start." I managed to do all that and climb down the steep rungs to the bottom and sit on the side of the feed chute. Someone brought water and I drank a slug of that. Dad said, "Enough for you up there today Mick. You get the rest of the day off." What can I say? Another close call. It sure as hell could have been a lot worse.

On a happier note, when very young I used to climb those same steel rungs on the silo steps, almost too far apart to get from one to the next, scared to death at first, with a pair of binoculars around my neck, and when I got to the top I would play army "scout" searching the whole area for Apaches, Cherokees, Cheyenne or Sioux. Sometimes I was on the lookout for North Koreans or Chinese Communists. This was when I wore the Army helmet liner brother Paul brought home from the service after the Korean War.

The morning chores also included walking south from the silo, past the big barn and on to the hog house to take care of the pigs. The hog house was located a little away from everything else, maybe due to the prevailing winds. I can recall at different times feeding corn, oats and particularly buttermilk to the pigs. A smelly, disagreeable place it was. The buttermilk was stored in a fifty-gallon barrel, and it always seemed like there were millions of flies around, and I would dip in the bucket and pour the stuff into the troughs below the swinging doors of each pen. And just outside was the "waller" that the hogs had to have in warm weather to cool off. This was a place into which we intentionally would run a hose to make mud to cool them off. It was a sight to behold to go out there and see thirty or forty hogs up to their ears or eyes in mud, grunting, snorting and enjoying themselves. The stench of the place was almost unbearable to me.

A Saturday affair: I can't decide which was more disagreeable to me, but as you might imagine, with all the diverse animals around and the diverse pens, a day of reckoning had to come for all. That was the day designated to clean out the chicken house, the barn (cattle, sheep or horses) or even worse, the hog house. More than likely it seemed to fall on Saturdays. I can recall over the years how the town kids looked forward to the weekend and Saturdays to picnics or ball games, but me and my buddy Luke Zimmerman would say on Monday, "Well, what kind of shit was it this weekend?" I shoveled chicken manure, hog manure, cow manure, sheep manure and even horse manure according to the occasion. Only a farm boy can tell you about the experience of working loose a shovelful of dung of some kind and see the steam come off it from the winter air, ah life. Dad had one of the old-fashioned manure spreaders, so we would pitch the stuff directly, if the aim was good, out the windows or the doors of the barn into the manure spreader. Once again, the odor was evil; often we had to clear out for a while, breathe a bit of fresh air before attacking it again. I tried to invent reasons to be busy on those Saturdays, and I got out of it sometimes, more often than Luke who seemed to do it every weekend. That was either because the Germans kept their barns cleaner than the Irish, or maybe they liked to shovel shit more than we did.

After the hog house it was on to the barn for more chores. When we had sheep, you had to go up above into the haymow and break open several bales of hay to toss down into the manger for the sheep. I can recall as a very small boy, well, maybe not so small, of riding the bigger ones much like a small horse, including getting tossed off. I received more than one lecture about that since it was entirely possible to injure the poor things, but what a fun time that was. We also broke open bales of hay for the cows and the horses. We only kept two or three milk cows at a time, the same with horses. Dad boarded horses for people in town, but that's another story.

The main chore in the barn was the milking. We always kept one or two milk cows for personal use. Eventually it became my chore to milk them. I have vivid recollections of those old cows, especially an old white one which eventually died after ingesting some metal or baling wire. Since we ran no dairy or sold to a dairy, we did not quite have the same standards as a dairy. You learned how to keep the milk clean, and most often it was, unless a stray fly would fall in and get wet and could not get out. But the barn was not exactly a sparkling place. We kept the place shoveled and swept, but it was not exactly "antiseptic". Flies abounded in summer. We had old wooden stanchions where we could lock the cow's head into place; we had metal leg chains, which were not always so easy to attach, to keep the cow from kicking the bucket over or from kicking us. I dodged many a blow. The milking stool was a t-shaped contraption, very simple, of two boards, perpendicular to each other, so you had to balance yourself, the bucket and be in the right vicinity to do the job.

I can recall town kids who would come to play would always want to help milk the cows. It never seemed a difficult task for us, but they seemed to have trouble getting the hang of it. I can only describe the motion as a slow squeezing and gentle pulling at the same time. Anyway, we had to spray the area in the summertime and spray the animals before milking because the flies were so bad. But that did not keep the old cow from constantly switching her tail. The personal hygiene of cattle being what it is, the tail was, let's say, hardened with fecal material (ain't that a nice word for "shit?") at its tip. That's the part that bats you in the face. So I devised a way to tie the tail in the sections of the metal leg chains, thus keeping her from switching me, but then the flies would drive her to distraction and I might still get a leg in my direction with spilt milk the result.

The other reason I often did not get a full pail of milk up to the house and the cream separator was the cats. Lots of them. We always had a cat or two for catching mice, but they proliferated as nothing else on the farm. I delighted in aiming a spurt of milk at their faces, watching them lick it all off and do it all over again. In spite of all the above we did seem to have enough milk and cream for home consumption, a good thing Dad was not into anything more than that, because we would have gone broke. A lingering memory was the cold, cold days when my hands were darn near frozen, sitting down to milk the old cow. I never considered it might hurt her worse than me.

Those icy mornings when the barnyard was semi frozen remind me of a story. I never wore work shoes to school and used rubber galoshes in the barn most of the time. But my buddy Luke one time had a pair of cowboy boots he wore doing chores, including the aforementioned cleaning out barns, and for some reason ended up wearing them to school one morning. It was one thing to be out in the frozen barnyard and another to come into a super-heated Kansas school building during the winter. The cow manure thawed, and he felt a bit like others were staring at him.

This is a good time to talk more about Luke, my good buddy for 12 years. I've told how we met in the yard of the Zimmerman's house east of the hospital. Luke and I had much in common, farm background, both Catholic, pretty typical kids, both fond of sports of all kinds and in having a good time. There would be many parallels in our twelve years growing up in Abilene. We were both very different. There were years when we were not close, but I believe in the final analysis there is more to bind us than separate us.

Eventually Luke and his family had to come into this account because faith, schooling and free time brought our families together. Our farm was one mile east of the city limits, its south edge on old Highway 40; the Zimmermans, as I said, on the very city limit, a bit south and west of us. The quickest way to get to their house to play when I was little was to walk down the lane, cut across the farm fields of Johnson's and on to the Zimmerman farm, and through the latter's corral. You could walk it all in about fifteen minutes. While still very little I remember playing over there, different games; I recall popcorn on cold days, all types of sports during season. One funny memory was in their house listening and singing along to the song "Buttons and Bows." Does that date me?

Later on I would work quite a bit for Luke's father, helping out on the farm in summertime. Hay baling mainly. I became a good friend of Grady, Luke's older brother who was in Caitlin's class in school.

Back to Luke and the friendship. There were some moments of rivalry, but really very few to my mind; things just seemed to always work out. We were both pretty good in academics, but I always thought he had more native brain matter and that it was more hard work on my part. Maybe it was just different talents in different directions, left brain - right brain, he more toward the sciences and me in humanities and languages.

Luke was a terrific all-around athlete; I was average at best. But we had literally years of contact through sports, little league baseball for many summers, diverse sports in grade school, junior high and high school. I've said I dropped out of sports during freshman year because of a serious concussion from football; Luke continued and dominated the school teams; he was the quarterback, the scoring guard in basketball, the leader. That bothered me very little I guess because I was resigned to the fact that I was just average at best in sports and since I was able to excel in other activities.

I had good roles in plays in 4-H and Jr. High, although I was never too serious about it. But I did have good luck in academics once I got serious about it about sophomore year in high school and in debate in high school. After the brain concussion in freshman football, I concentrated on debate team. I enjoyed public speaking and the whole debate routine. I was president of the local 4-H club and that involved lots of speaking opportunities, I did some declamation contests in junior high, but the best practice was as student council president in high school when I would introduce all assemblies and was called upon for speaking on all kinds of occasions.

But back to debate. Our debate teams had a good tradition, and we placed in the state tournament my junior year and won first place senior year, my role being fairly significant. I always put that in balance to Luke's athletic achievements since none of our sports teams ever came close to winning state, not his fault for sure. We both were popular with the girls, and that also never created problems. It seemed to turn out in Abilene that before you were done you had dated what seemed like every cute girl in town some time or other during those years. I think I tell somewhere Luke's and my Mom getting together and "suiting us up" for the first junior high dance, a purple corduroy sport coat, grey flannel slacks, pink shirt and tie! Luke will come into the farm story a good deal. I figure you never have more than three or four "good" friends in life, and I count him as one.

Back to the chores. Once or twice I neglected the milking. Imagine a milk cow that must be milked twice a day after a time is missed. I caught holy hell for that. I got lots of spankings and whippings, but I vividly recall the day when I was old enough and fast enough that Dad could not catch me to give me a whipping for such times when I "blew off" the chores.

14

MICK, THE PALOMINOS, JOYS AND SORROWS

So much seemed to be going on in those chores years. As I've already said, Dad was a real "horse trader" dating back to his boyhood days in Nebraska at the end of the 19th century. Dad only went to 8th grade; he was needed to work on the farm as were all the farm boys then. His family had to make a living with horses, so he learned quickly. I still think he maintained you could look in the horse's mouth at the teeth and find out all you needed to know. (Is this where we learned "Don't look a gift horse in the mouth?") I was a dunce on the farm with not understanding all the technical biological goings-on but knew when a stud stallion or breeding bull was ready to get to work. I loved our two horses, both Palominos, the momma mare a beautiful brown (is it "sorrel"?) with a white blaze on her forehead, thus her name "Blaze." The mare's foal was a filly, a standard colored golden palomino with white "socks" above her hooves (she looked like Roy Rogers' Trigger in the movies). In the old milk barn there were old leather harnesses and such, must have been from Nebraska days, mostly filled with cracks from aging, but there was a shiny new saddle and bridle, bit and blankets for riding. Dad kept all the latter in good order with regular oiling and such.

That's where my story comes in. When I was about twelve or thirteen, along with all the chores I've already described, Dad said one day, "Why don't you take the filly up to bring in the cattle and sheep from the north 80? I'll saddle her up for you." You've got to know why I hesitated. Earlier that summer in a fit of who knows what I had saddled the filly, got on her, gently nudged her sides with my boots (not cowboy, but farm work boots) and she took off. We moved from what I think they call a canter or maybe a trot (hell, I'm no expert) and when I nudged her more, into a real gallop. I know when she was "full out" there was no bouncing up and down, but a smooth ride. We ended going over the plowed wheat field up along the terraces toward the pond, and I think part of the time at full speed. That was when it happened. On the way back down to the alfalfa field and the barn, for whatever reason, the damned horse stopped suddenly, maybe she was spooked by a snake or something, and I flew over the top, flipping over in the air and landing none too gently on my back side.

The gods must have been smiling upon the farm boy, because not only did I not have any broken bones, but really was not badly bruised, just maybe stunned. And chagrined. I think I muttered, "You damned horse, that's the last time you'll do that to me." Or whatever, but not much bravado, I walked the filly back to the barn, unsaddled it, and never rode it again the rest of the summer.

That is, until Dad's "suggestion." I guess it was an "invite" not to be turned down. So Dad saddled the horse that afternoon, maybe 5:00 o'clock, and encouraging me, said, "Mick, give it a try. I think you'll do all right."

I don't know if horses can sense when you are afraid of them, but I was, and I think it did. We rode out of the big corral west of the barn, alongside the windbreak and then into full pasture with the buffalo grass. All was going well, riding in a trot, and me on the filly, we quickly reached the end of the main pasture up the hill, rode through the gate in the wire fence and on up into the north 80. As luck would have it, the damned cattle were in the far northeast corner, grazing up north of the pond. And the stupid sheep were in a huddle on the northwest end of the 80. I figured the cattle would be easier, so I rode over to them and began to shoo them back up the hill to the gate. Have you ever seen those old cows run, it's kind of a hoot, the rear end swaying back and forth and the teats the same (most of the cows had calves and thus big udders). The calves were the problem, no discipline to them, like herding cats. But eventually I got the whole bunch up the hill and shouting, got them headed down the south pasture and the hill, the barn in sight far away.

That left the sheep. By now I'm getting a little saddle sore and not enjoying the ride that much. I forgot, of some but little help was our Border Collie, Lady, running along behind the sheep, nipping at their back legs. Border Collies are supposed to have the natural genes for herding, but the problem was Lady did not have any method to her madness and would end up scattering the sheep. That left me and the filly to try and round them up. This particular time they ended up scattered over the entire north 80, me pissed off and yelling at the damned dog and finally saying the hell with it. I turned Blaze around and heading back to the south pasture where the cattle were ambling down the hill toward the corral. Once you got them started, they were pretty much on "automatic" mainly because they were thirsty and were headed to the only stock tank located in the corral.

Dad was waiting and had a bit of a smile on his face, and said, "Where's the rest?" I told him my sad tale and moaned and groaned about being sore, but he said, "They've got to come in; Mick, you know there are coyotes all around. We can't let them stay up there and they won't come in alone." Grudgingly I said, "Okay, but lock Lady up somewhere so she don't spook 'em." I turned the filly around and we started all over again. If you stand in the stirrups your butt doesn't hurt so much, so that was how I managed to get me and the horse back up to the north 80. Sure enough, the sheep were bunched back together, so this time with a lot of back and forth and yelling, I got them headed through the gate and headed down to the barn, them following the fence on the west side. Gradually the filly and me got them back down in the corral, the gate locked behind them, and me unsaddling the filly, giving her a pat on the head and a couple of handfuls of oats from the feed bin. We were back on good terms.

Little did I know, but that would be the last time when I felt like a cowboy, or at least a farm boy doing cowboy stuff. It was early spring, the grass turning green and coming up. And there was a heavy dew on the ground. I had finished eating breakfast at the kitchen table and was rinsing my dishes in the sink with the north window. I could see Dad was out doing chores, north of the silo. And the filly was cavorting and running through the meadow north of the granary out toward the pasture, frisky as ever, a beautiful sight. I didn't see it happen, but she suddenly pulled up lame, silent and hobbling. Dad yelled, "Mick get out here," and I put on a jacket and hat and ran out of the house up toward the silo where he was standing alone, a pitchfork in his hand, just looking at the filly.

The broken bone was sticking way out of her leg, just above the knee. Dad saw me run up, came over and said, "Mick, we've got to put her out of her misery. Go into the house and the stairway to the basement where the guns are and bring me a rifle. Now, get going." I ran into the house, slamming the door to the mud room, went down the stone steps to the gun rack and there was a moment of panic – no rifles in sight! Shit, Joe had gone hunting the day before with some high school buddies and must have taken them all, the single shot and the 22 Special.

"Dad, they're ain't no rifles. Joe must have 'em." He swore under his breath, then said, "Bring the 12 gauge and a couple of shells. They're in a box on a shelf by the stairway." I ran back, got the gun and shells, and ran back to the silo and handed them to Dad. He said, "Mick, why don't you go back to the house. It might be better for you not to see this. It'll be over quick, and she'll never know what hit her." It was an order.

I head the shot, just one and looking out the north kitchen window saw the filly crumple to the ground. Disobeying Dad, and with Mom now looking on sadly, I ran back to the silo. The young horse had a hole the size of a half-dollar in the middle of her forehead and blood was slowing pouring out of that hole. Dad had the shotgun in one arm, looked at me, now in tears, came over and put his other arm around me. "Mick, it had to be done. They only do surgeries on the fancy racehorses; the cost is prohibitive, and we just can't and don't do it on the farm." I don't know where it came from, but the words popped into my head: "They shoot horses, don't they?" Now I understood.

I remembered the filly bucking me off, but also those times when she didn't and we rode like the wind along the terraces, her mane blowing in that wind. And me feeling exhilarated and scared at the same time, the only time in my life I really felt like I had had a full-out fast ride. And I remembered the times in the pasture with the cattle, the sheep, Lady and her antics. The last memory, not a good one, was the horrible, stinking smell of the rendering truck and two men who came and using a rope and pulley, dragged the filly into the back of the truck, put up the door, locked it and drove off. What I didn't imagine at the time was how Dad felt, realizing when I thought about it, how important horses were to him his entire life. We never bought or had another horse. I guess Dad could not bear breeding the old mare again.

15

JOE, CAITLIN, MICK, 4-H DAYS, WILHELMINA AND GUS

Growing up on a small farm in Dickinson County left no choice but for all of the kids in our family to be in 4-H. I think we all participated to some degree in scouting, me only a year or two in the Cubs, but that was basically for the town kids. 4-H was the way you did it on the farm. But we had a curious situation, living so close to town. We were all members of the local club which belonged to the town of Abilene, the Abilene Aggies. I do not recall if I ever had a choice in the matter, if I was asked if I wanted to be in 4-H. I just followed along in Caitlin's and Joe's footsteps. Keep in mind that Paul was fifteen years older than myself, "grown up" and working in business in a nearby town most of my childhood years on the farm; he may have done a lot of this, but I don't know.

Joe and Caitlin both excelled in 4-H on both the local and state levels, participating in livestock projects, animal judging, but also in sewing and cooking in Caitlin's case and in woodworking with Joe.

I believe the 4-H meetings were held once a month, always in the city hall in Eisenhower park in the fairgrounds and adjacent to the local armory and the old CCC baseball stadium. I can never remember a time when one of us was not an important officer in the club. Both Joe and Caitlin were role models for me in later years, although you never put it in those terms or thought about it that way then. Joe was president for a couple of terms, Caitlin secretary. I later was president during my time. There were so many instances when I followed in Joe's footsteps, in 4-H, in academics and in sports to some extent, and in Paul's when it came to debate in high school. I believe the club had a sergeant at arms, a song leader, secretary, treasurer, vice president and president. Also there was the customary reporter - there were always the mandatory reports for the "Abilene Reflector Chronicle," the local small town newspaper dominated by one Harold D. Bushmill who definitely represented the "town" opinion and the right side of the tracks folks, the country club set. All this was not consciously complained about by most kids I knew who were largely unaware of class in those days, but this was probably not the case with their more aware parents. Suffice to say, in Kansas farm country and even more, in Eisenhower country, the political slant was always conservative or moderate Republican. What else? We were an Eisenhower town! That was a good thing.

The 4-H meetings were a social situation for us kids. Because it was a town club, the members were by and large not "country" and had more of a small-town makeup. I believe Abilene had 7000 people at the time. For whatever reason, there was a tone, a lack of "country" and a bit more sophistication to the club. I can remember we started the meeting with the 4-H pledge: "I pledge my heart to greater loyalty, my head to greater thinking, my hands to greater service and my health to better living, for my club, my community and my country." Then came the inevitable songs to be sung with great gusto or giggling by some of us: "You Are My Sunshine," "Sunflower State," "Tell Me Why" and many other rousing ditties, most seeming pretty corny to me. Then came old business, then new business, then the treasurer's report. It was the closest thing to the atmosphere of an old-fashioned town meeting I have ever experienced; there truly was a democratic tone. And parliamentary procedure ruled the day. Each year the county had a 4-H Model Meeting Day, and clubs would compete with the goal to hold the niftiest "model" meeting according to correct procedures. It seemed like the Aggies always did well along that line.

Another of our fortés was the little plays clubs would put on in a county competition, all on the same day, an entire Saturday. All the clubs in the county would compete. The Aggies were outstanding in my time. My brother Paul who had considerable experience in acting, drama and music in high school, and you got to be known for such things in the small towns, was our director for many years. I can recall the fun and the excitement each year when the club would compete for the prize and most often win it. Later on I became a regular cast member, with some success as I recall. Drama was a big extra-curricular activity in junior high and high school in those days, and I got the lead in two or three of the plays, including one or two in 4-H. I can remember one title – "Auggie Evans Private Eye." I cannot for the life of me remember where they dug up those plays, but somebody must have done some research. Anyway, it was great fun. In 4-H days it seemed easy to memorize the lines to those plays and also to dramatic readings we did in speech class in public school.

I can recall one of the highlights of meetings on summer nights was to hurry out of the meeting and go over to the ballpark where the Jr. Legion or someone would be in the middle of a night baseball game. And often someone would be selling homemade pie, cake and ice cream outside the band shell; it seems like a big piece of chocolate cake and a bowl of homemade ice cream were about 25 to 50 cents. My mouth still waters when I think of that.

There were other fun moments of 4-H: the "4-H Day" or "Project Day," generally in midsummer when we would all pile in the back of a big open bed truck and drive all around the county to the different farms to see each other's projects, the best part of the day being the great picnic afterwards out at Eisenhower Park.

At our place, and I was excited, they saw our sheep, chickens and my Sears Gilt Wilhelmina. The sheep were in the barn yard as were our two palomino horses. Anxious for petting or treats, the momma Palomino came up to my sister Caitlin, ready to pet her, and instead took a big chomp out of her stomach. Caitlin screamed, so did some other people, and we were embarrassed our 4-H animals would not "be decent" on this important occasion. Luckily, the bite barely broke the skin and Caitlin survived to enjoy and swimming and picnic that followed in Eisenhower Park.

The food was the usual rural fare, fried chicken, potato salad, farm tomatoes, corn on the cob I think, cake, pie, and ice-cold watermelon. We also drank iced tea or soft drinks (no appetite whetted for beer yet in those days). I forgot, part of it all too was we went swimming in the big public pool in the park before eating; swimming too soon after eating was feared in those days. (About this time on the farm I would pour hot water on a thermometer and show Mom it was 70 degrees, warm enough for all of us to go swimming.) There were the baseball games later on in the evening. And memories are vague, but I think a lot of early teen age flirting took place then too. All I know is my memories are great. But we had fun. I guess some people had more fun than others. The teen age pregnancy was still really frowned upon; the girl generally just "disappeared" for a few months and maybe or maybe not returned to school. Babies were given up for adoption in the great majority of cases. And everyone knew the "good' and "bad" girls, and the "good" girls who were bad sometimes, and how all you needed to do was get a couple of beers down the girl, and how you better have a condom in your billfold. It was all pretty much folklore, or you might say, "bullshit!" This did not at all coincide with being Catholic, naive, and scared shitless of the consequences if you were in my shoes.

This leads me to other animals, the pets on the farm and the 4-H animals. We always had a pet of some kind or other, but in a very different sense than pets in the city. A pet had to also have some primary use or function; there had to be some good out of it. So, our dogs were always work dogs, at least to some degree. We did have a little terrier; Ginger I think was its name; I was so tiny I can hardly remember. But I do know that when Ginger died, we had a doggy funeral and buried the animal on the north side of the barn near the corral with a wooden cross to mark the spot.

I remember better our beautiful Collie "Carlo," a wonderful farm dog that went with Dad to the fields each day, loping alongside the little Ford tractor Dad used to farm an entire half section of land. The dog would follow the tractor or whatever stirring up rabbits. But its life ended tragically, like most of the animals I remember loving on the farm.

I can recall one time when Carlo came home, not really seriously sick, but just below par. We discovered a spent bullet in its hide, shot perhaps accidentally, perhaps not, by a hunter's bullet. The wound was not bleeding and healed shortly, but Carlo's end came soon after that. One day while keeping Dad company in the field (this day Dad was mowing hay and had a mower attached to the rear of the tractor with a cycle blade running to the side), the dog ran too close once too often and the mower of course clipped its legs. Dad quickly grabbed a hammer out of the tractor toolbox and put the poor animal out of its misery with a quick blow to the head. But a more faithful companion he never had, and although I was very young, I mourned old Carlo.

The next farm dog was the one I recall best, a black and white Border Collie called "Lady." Lady was a good dog. All our pets lived on table scraps and their own initiative as hunters. We never purchased dog food in town. Lady often would come home with a rabbit from the field, and it was just expected that she would fend for herself most of the time. She had good blood from the Border Collie line, but never did have the proper training to go along with it. Yet instinct took her a long way, an adventure I already told. I recall particularly when Dad ran sheep for a few years and the dog would run along behind, nipping their hind feet, helping to herd them into the corral. The same with cattle, when I used to go up to the pasture with the Ford tractor to bring in the cattle, Lady would accompany me, a joy for a young boy. She did not have any particular shelter during bad weather but would craw under the front porch of the house in inclement weather. But never was a farm dog allowed inside the house, no matter what.

Lady had one fault — she loved to bark at cars coming up the driveway or in the parking area in front of the house. And occasionally she would get all the way down the lane and bark at cars as they passed on old Highway 40. That was how she met her end, hit by a car she barked at and chased.

There were also the cats, anywhere from two or three up to over a dozen, they seemed to proliferate on the farm. They lived largely from hunting rodents, small mice in the barns, table scraps and some milk. They got plenty of the latter whenever I milked the cows; only later did I realize the loss to Dad when I brought far less milk than actually given by the cow to the house, having either given it to or squirted the cats in the barn.

The 4-H animals came to be a sort of pet, though not in the same sense as the dogs or cats. There was the most famous, Wilhelmina, the Sears Gilt. Sears funded a program locally in which a 4-Her received a gilt, sent it to be bred and when it farrowed, could keep all but one gilt of the new litter which was passed on to the next boy or girl. They were Durocs in my day, a deep red or rust colored, or Hampshires, black with white stripe along the back. I can remember getting mine with the promise of a good project, getting her ready for the county fair and also making some money. This involved feeding the animal and particularly preparing it for the fair. We would arrive at the latter sometime in late summer, but the animal's time was competitive with summer baseball, farm work and other affairs. I can recall making a short board about two by three feet, out of thin plywood, painting our name on it and the name of the local 4-H club "Abilene Aggies". The idea was to practice moving the pig around a small area or enclosure with the help of this board and a long stick (maybe like a broom handle) in the other hand. The idea was to show off the pig's best qualities, whatever they were, to the judge of the competition. I know you did not want the pig to be too fat, too skinny and you had to have it clean, so there were faucets and a wash area or pen at the fairgrounds in the pig barn. We are talking serious business here, but I was serious only up to a point. I had much more fun having balloon fights, playing, flirting with the girls and eating delicious hamburgers at the outdoor food stands at the fairgrounds, great days! I cannot recall but I think my Sears Gilt won a red ribbon standing for second class. And I know I had more than one pig so I may be confusing them.

We never had a pickup truck while Dad had the farm; the main reason I think was money. Instead we had a trailer of sorts we could put sides on and haul one or two animals, towing with the old car, a late 1940s Plymouth. That's how Wilhelmina and others made it to the fair. I can't recall if it was she or not, but I did sell one pig in the annual 4-H sale making a few bucks.

The most memorable time with Wilhelmina was later on in her illustrious career. Breeding time came, so we loaded her into the same rickety trailer and took her down the road to visit the local stud hog. It came time to pick her up; the owner of the stud hog had called saying she was ready to come home. I remember the trip home yet today. Mom and Dad were in the car, but I was driving. We were heading home, having crossed the Smokey Hill river bridge south and east of town. The pig somehow uprooted the gate of the trailer. I was tooling along and happened to look in the rear-view mirror and saw this cloud of dust on the road behind the car and trailer. Wilhelmina had literally "hit the road" in a cloud of dust and was rolling over and over. By the time we braked the car and backed up, she was running lickety-split off in the middle of a milo field by the river. I guess she was heading back to her lover boy. We spent the next hour, and it was quite cold as I recall, sometime in the fall, chasing that damned fool hog across the milo field. We finally caught it, had no rope in the car or truck but did have some baling wire in the trunk (no farmer would be without it) and managed to get her back in the trailer and home.

Evidently she was unhurt because several months later she farrowed a huge litter of pigs, but Wilhelmina did not end up with a happy family situation. The hog decided to farrow on the coldest night of the winter, well below zero. Dad was not at home for this was the winter he was in Florida doing carpentry work to keep things going. But at about two in the morning Mom woke me up and said we had better be checking on the hog. We went out and tried to save the pigs. Wilhelmina had sixteen, I think. All seemed to go well so we went back to the house, still in the middle of the night. The next morning when we went out to the hog house, the scene was a disaster: there were frozen pigs all up and down the alleyway, strewn all over the hog house, and only three alive. Most had crept out from under the heat lamp that was in the middle of the farrowing pen, down into the feeding trough, and under the swinging door that separated it from the alleyway. That disaster marked my last experience I recall with pigs. Wilhelmina herself was either eventually butchered or sold at market. I cannot recall exactly when, but we knew it was bound to happen sooner or later.

The entire experience with the farm animals, especially the 4-H animals is a delicate subject with me yet. Not that I never liked or resented the work associated with them, but I never did seem to have a talent for it, never really got the hang of it. I suppose I learned something from it all, but darned little. For sure, nothing from my Dad's great knowledge rubbed off on me. I could do the chores, knew how to take care of the animals' feed, but never really understood the biological part of it including the breeding. Not that I was ignorant of the main facts of breeding, but I did not understand a lot of the whys and wherefores and whens. And it was not indifference as much as it was an absolutely untalented area for me. My life seems to run to those extremes. I think I have written how I would become almost physically sick when I had to play the role of "gofer" when Dad worked on machinery; such was my lack of interest and absolute lack of inclination toward anything mechanical.

But I do laugh when I think of the cloud of dust in the road or me trying to herd a hog around at the fair or of Gus Goose, a main character in it all.

Gus Goose and the geese. Gus was the "most unforgettable character" of the farm animals. It all goes back to my early teen years when I became excited with the idea of raising geese for the 4-H project. I would start out small, but I figured that about 3000 geese would be the goal. We reached about 24 I think, but that was enough! I'll tell you about the great enterprise. I can recall like yesterday Dad going into town and getting the goose eggs. I think he used chicken hens to sit on them and hatch them. Anyway, it started with two or three geese and a gander, of the Grey Toulouse variety. Little by little we ended with about 24. The geese had no specific place to be or be found, but were allowed to roam the farmyard, corral, and fields near the farmhouse. There is a scotch whiskey, Ballantine's I believe, which advertised for some time using white geese as "watchdogs" for the distillery. Ours could have applied for the job. Any unusual noise, any stranger or car coming up the lane and it sounded like a migration of Canadas, honking by all sizes and shapes of the geese. If especially excited they would all set off running and a few would actually fly a bit across the barnyard.

The geese would nest each spring, and one fine day the goose would appear with several little goslings trailing behind her. We decided to help out and raise the little ones in the warm house (it must have been early spring because it was still quite cold outside). The place was a corner in the warm kitchen. A cardboard box was placed in the corner which contained plenty of fresh newspaper for them, and we gave them plenty of water and feed. So I was in business. They were so darned cute, small, cuddly, warm, and just kind of cooing at that age. We soon discovered that the babies could not walk properly on the slick linoleum of the kitchen floor. But if you took tiny strips of cloth and tied their legs together, they could stand up and get along just fine. Fun times.

But live and learn on the farm. Sometime later we saw these geese now grown weaving drunkenly all over the barn yard like they'd been eating sour mash instead of chicken mash. It took a while, but it turns out something in the formula was actually blinding the poor things. Once we figured it out, we saved the rest. But it did rather inhibit the flock size.

The geese loved a rainy day, and that is when we discovered Gus Goose, the big gander, and his wonderful personality. One day during a particularly heavy rain, the kind that came with rivulets of water running all across the yard, we found him rolling a five-gallon bucket along the ground, pushing it along with his beak. What prompted the behavior I cannot say, but every time it rained, he was out there with the bucket. Gus came to be the true leader of the flock, the head gander. In the haymow of our old-fashioned barn there was a wooden floor, and in the center, we had some time ago put up a basketball goal, so I played continually for years, certainly all through junior high and high school. At one end of this floor there was a door which could be slid open, and the view outside was a nice one, encompassing the farm to the south, all the way to and beyond the highway. At that time I either rode a bicycle or walked to school in good weather. I can recall many an afternoon while still walking along the highway heading for the lane and home to the farmhouse, I would see all the geese, with Gus at their head, blissfully gazing out the haymow door as if surveying all their domain. They never voluntarily flew out that door, but I chased them out a time or two, just to see what would happen. They could not really fly long distances but would flap their wings and make it safely to the ground.

On one of those occasions home from school, I went out to the barn to play basketball, and when I came into the haymow from the door on the other end, Gus was perfectly balanced up on the basketball left on the floor. I ask myself today, now at age 18, was it my imagination? I swear I saw it. Gus was only beginning to come into his glory. In later times, and no thanks to me, he won the Grand Champion Purple ribbon in the gander category of the Dickinson County Free Fair in Abilene, his crowning glory. His end, not different from lesser geese, was the dinner table. That was after my original dream of a flock of three thousand had ebbed with the passing of time. I do recall in this instance that I would not partake of that meal.

What remains of the goose chronicle are memories of incredible noise, a real racket when they would get started, and goose doodoo all over the place. And that strange behavior.

I guess I was a rascal, don't know if there was a genuine cruel streak, or if that was just what farm kids did. I would unnecessarily pull at the dogs' ears or tails or pick up a kitty cat and toss it into the air to see if it would land on its feet, which it always did. I cannot explain the how or why I did such things other than just plain devilment, and nothing ever carried past that early age.

16

IKE EISENHOWER, FAIRS, RODEOS AND CIRCUSES

And that memory of the fair and 4-H animals brings me to another important time related to 4-H. It was 1952. General Dwight Eisenhower came to Abilene to launch his campaign for presidency of the United States; there was a big parade down Buckeye and then west on 3rd street to the city park where he would actually give the speech. Local 4-H clubs created floats for the parade. I played a young Eisenhower (this even before I shared Ike's semi-baldness, coming on as early as senior year in high school). During the speech in Eisenhower Park the rain poured. Afterwards I jumped down from the stands, ran up to the Eisenhowers' black limousine, stuck my head in the window and said "Hi Mami, hi Ike." I think I remember his smile.

That brings me to the Rodeo, always associated with the fair. It was a big affair, one of the most exciting times of the year for us farm folks; the official name was "The Dickinson County Free Fair and Rodeo." On several occasions I drove a tractor from one of the local dealerships in the fair-rodeo parade and got comps or free tickets for the rodeo. Another way to get a ticket was to volunteer to lead an animal in the livestock parade before the rodeo performance. Imagine a leather halter, a huge heifer or steer a few hundred pounds bigger than you are, trying to avoid putting your foot in cow pies, and you've got the picture. But I did garner several tickets to the rodeo that way.

The "comps" or coupons were issued in varied colors, each color designated for a specific night of the rodeo. On the nights we did not have a "legitimate" ticket, me and my buddies would sneak through a hole in the old outfield fence and hopefully show the ticket taker the right colored coupon and we were in! I think all this took place during the National Anthem.

There were great memories of the rodeo itself - the "grand entry" with all the cowboys, cowgirls, and the judges on their horses, riding at top speed around the arena. It all was very exciting. We intently watched and kept score of all the events - bareback bronco riding, calf roping, saddle back bronco riding, and my favorite, brahma bull riding. I yet today remember one behemoth all grey in color, the bull "Joe Lewis." Then there were the brave clowns who would protect the riders after they either jumped off or were thrown by the bull. The clowns would hide in a barrel right in front of the bull. And they would swap ribald commentary with the rodeo announcer, all I guess "arranged" ahead of time. But once again, it was great fun. I can remember the specialty acts in between events - the pretty girls in sequins doing "Roman Riding," that is, riding, standing with one leg on each of two horses. Makes me think of the country song "Everything that glitters is not gold."

There were other events at the rodeo grounds. There was "The Joey Chitwood Auto Daredevil Show" and a night of smashing up cars in the local demolition derbies.

On one occasion the rodeo merited the Grand Ole' Opry show with no less than Roy Acuff! This was BIG TIME for Abilene.

The fair alongside the rodeo. In the "good old days" both events, the Dickinson County Free Fair and Rodeo, were held the same week and complemented each other. Some of the events and moments were:

－ Throwing water balloons from the top of the old CCC stadium

- The watermelons we tossed from the top of the stadium
- The great hamburgers cooked at the outdoor food stands
- The gypsies who stole eggs from the 4-H poultry exhibit
- The "carnies" and the great times we had at the carnival, flirting with girls upon occasion. There were the rides including the Ferris wheel, bumper cars and the like. There was a "freak" show with all kinds of aberrations, and the "girlie show" for the older guys. And you could easily spend and lose your hard-earned money from farm chores with the crooked or nigh impossible games at the carnival. I recall one in particular - a sort of mechanical crane with a tiny bucket; you cranked the crane to try to "fish out" silver dollars. And there was the ring toss where you would toss amazingly tiny rings to try to land on the tops of coke bottles.
- Sterl Hall and all the inside 4-H exhibits: cooking, pies, cakes, and sewing
- The stock barns and the animal exhibits - cattle, hogs, chickens, geese, or sheep. I recall the "herding board" I used to show Wilhelmina my Sears' Gilt, this after washing, and brushing the animal. And of course the day came to part with her as a result of the 4-H livestock sale. And there was my disastrous participation in the animal poultry judging contest.
- Ducks, chicken and geese. My 4-H project, the Grey Toulouse Gus Goose, became county grand champion.
- The weather at the fair/rodeo brought a noticeable coolness, a sign that SCHOOL WAS ABOUT TO START! So that meant school clothes, and for the O'Briens that meant for the most part J.C. Penney's and maybe Howard Keel's on a very, very special occasion. I think the main item was blue jeans, and Penney's brand was Dickies if I'm not mistaken. I was so skinny a kid that they hung on me anyway, and I can remember a photo with my belt tightened to hold them up and the jeans wrinkled around it. T-shirts were also acceptable, white as I recall, but I know I had colored shirts as well.

72

I can't recall, but I guess tennis shoes were the norm. All this would change in junior high and especially high school. Shirts became a bit dressier, shoes were brown or black loafers, and I think some kind of dress slacks were worn to school, especially on the occasions when I had to speak to introduce lyceums, etc. as president of student council senior year. When we did wear tennis shoes, they were high top. A related matter was schoolbooks. I can't recall where we got schoolbooks, but I think at a downtown music store, the same place I would buy my first guitar at about age 14, a Stella steel string.

Related to the fair and rodeo was another huge event for our whole town and community – the arrival of the circus! There were two moments, the first when I was really tiny, sometime between 5 and 10 years old – the Barnum and Baily Three-Ring Circus. It was everything a boy, especially a farm boy, could want – the circus arrived with the Union Pacific Train. We all went down to see it, the horses, the camels and the huge elephants, and then the lion and tiger cages. I don't know how they got everything out to the site, the fairgrounds north of the CCC stadium and rodeo pavilion. We watched a time or two as they put up the big top, the biggest tent I'd ever seen, big muscled guys with no shirts on swinging huge sledgehammers on iron stakes to hold it down. Funny, I don't remember the circus itself so much except that it was frustrating because there were different things going on in each ring. The scariest part was the high wire and trapeze artists, "death-defying" feats. And lots of cotton candy.

Maybe more memorable, because it had to come later, was the Clyde Beatty circus, still three rings, but smaller than Barnum and Baily and coming into town in big trucks. The highlight was Clyde himself in the lion and tiger cage, just a small chair and a whip. We were sure he was going to be eaten alive! More cotton candy and excitement. I'm sure all us kids, Caitlin, Joe and me, and probably Mom and Dad and Grandma too.

17

MOLLY AND THE BIRDS

After all that talk of 4-H and the animals, I've got to talk about Mom who had a great love of flowers, birds and just being out of doors. She always had some flowers out each spring, this aside from the annuals. There were beautiful lilacs north of the house, tulips for a short time each spring, jonquils, lots of multi-colored iris, and lots of roses. There was a slight incline in the yard to the north of the farmhouse; the mound was above the storm cellar, another creepy place for me, used to store potatoes and theoretically protect us all from Kansas tornadoes. Mom used this area and worked off and on for years there on her rock garden with all kinds of flowers and plants. I have the impression she received little help with all that, not much cooperation on the part of the kids. But I know she loved it.

Mom loved the birds, the sounds of each, and tried to instill an appreciation of them in us, again not very successfully at the time. But the Mockingbird and my favorite song of the Meadowlark were garnered from her lessons. The most beautiful birds were the red Cardinal which stayed into the winter and would eat seed or scraps we put out, or the Blue Jay, a feisty bird along the line of the Mockingbird which would play with and fool the cats we always had around the farm. We also had Turtle Doves and Whippoorwills with their plaintive song.

As a general rule I was not particularly attuned to wildlife. We had pheasants in the fields, but generally saw them when on drives in the country, along the two-lane highways or gravel roads. Once in a while an old hoot owl would appear in the trees out by the barn. There were lots of cottontail rabbits in the fields as well as the prairie jack rabbit. I can recall a time when we would go crazily bouncing over the pastures in a pickup truck with a spotlight and net to catch the jacks and get a premium for them from the coursing park where they used them live for greyhound racing. My best hunting shot ever was a long shot of a lone jack on a ridge after a winter snowstorm, went in one eye and out the other, a grizzly affair I'm not too proud of. It was a good shot though.

We would see an occasional garter snake or bull snake (one big one wrapped itself around the telephone wire entering the house and we had to knock it down with a hoe), but I never did see a prairie rattler and am not sure they were in our part of the country. Dad used to talk about the blue snake or Blue Racer and tell tales of them chasing you in the field. I don't know yet if that is true.

I can remember the excitement in 1951 when there was flooding around the valley with the high water from the Smokey Hill River south of Abilene. I do not know how or why, but we had several deer in our upland pasture that summer, and it was fun to see them easily leap the fences that had barbed wire on top for keeping cattle in.

We heard coyotes, but rarely saw them. I can only remember once or twice seeing them in the daytime, once while riding the school bus north of town. Antelope I never saw on the farm, but only on those times on the western plains of Kansas or eastern Colorado on rare trips to Colorado Springs or Denver.

There would be an occasional possum, and one time we had a badger making mounds up in the wheat field near the pond; I believe it was either trapped or poisoned. That reminds me of the bounty money the county had put on such animals, including gophers. It must have been a dollar or two per animal. Brother Joe spent a lot of time and energy setting traps out in the alfalfa fields, in the mounds and tunnels they made in the fields. He did not get rich. They could absolutely ruin a good, level field in a short time. So it was a declared war.

18

BRINGING IN THE CATTLE – MICK AND THE TRACTOR

There was still another thing to come with the chores; this was after I no longer could ride a horse up to bring in the cattle. That still left the chore, but this time maybe more fun, lots more. Dad would let me drive the little Ford tractor up to "get the cattle." I had been driving it for a couple of years, maybe since I was twelve. Farm boys learned early because the tractor was used for all that field work and plowing stuff. And a young boy's imagination, at least in my case, came into play. Too young to have a real car, much less the money to buy one, the Ford became my hot-rod. I would drive it in 4th gear, top speed maybe 25 miles per hour, up the road in the middle of the pasture, this on the way up to get the cattle. I loved to pull the throttle gismo to max and fly over a terrace, actually putting the tractor a bit into the air. The Ford's front wheels were spread apart, so it really was hard to get it out of kilter. It only turned out bad just this one time.

I had it at full throttle and went flying over a terrace near one of the water-ways Dad had put in the pasture to stop erosion. Somehow or other, I think the front tire hit a gopher hole on the way down, and the tractor flipped over, throwing me out of the tractor seat, into the air, and landing with a thud and rolling along the ground. I was dazed, and my arm and left leg hurt like hell. And blood was running down my face. I could see the tractor had slid to a stop a few yards away, on its side, the right front wheel still spinning. I hurt so bad I thought maybe I was dying. I was way up on the top of the pasture hill, out of sight and shouting distance of the corral, farm buildings and the house. It was starting to get dark and I was crying from the pain. I couldn't move.

As it was starting to get dark, I saw the headlights of the old Plymouth coming fast up the road in the middle of the pasture. Mom and Dad must have realized I should have long ago been back and that the cattle had meandered on down to the corral. They roared up to where they saw the tractor, then me, and ran over to where I was lying on the ground, writhing in pain. Dad said, "No time to waste; we'll try to get you into the back seat and on up to the hospital." I just remember groaning and being totally woozy from then on. On the way, there was no talk at all. Dad drove us up to the emergency entrance of old Memorial Hospital, Mom jumped out and told the attending nurse what had happened. Soon there was a stretcher on a cart with wheels and two male nurses on either end. They slid me onto it and wheeled me up to what I guess was emergency. There was a shot for the pain, a nurse with a hot washcloth washing off my face and I heard someone say, we need to get him down to x-ray right away. Whatever they gave me put me out. That's all I know.

Don't know when, but I woke up in bed with my left leg in a cast from my ankle up to the top of my thigh, and another cast from my fingers to my elbow. And it hurt like hell. Mom was on one side of the bed, Dad on the other. She said, "They want to keep you over night and you my fine young scamp are going to learn to walk with crutches." Dad just said, "What happened?"

We had a saying then – "The jig's up." No getting out of this easy. A tractor doesn't roll over on its side, especially the little Fords, if you're going at a regular speed. So it was time for that ole' Catholic confession (we had all been taught to never but never lie). I'm not sure if anything I said made sense, but I mumbled that I was just having some fun on the way up to get the cows, was maybe driving a little too fast over one of the terraces. Dad said, "What were you doing way over there? That terrace is on the other side of the pasture, away from the road up to the gate and the north 80 with the cattle. It's time you 'fessed up.'" "I guess maybe I was going a little too fast and was just 'jumping' the terrace. I'd done it before, so it didn't seem like any problem to me. I'm sorry Dad and Mom; it was stupid, and I've learned my lesson."

They released me from the hospital the next day, and Dad and Mom came to pick me up, me now on crutches. It was about five long weeks until they changed it to a walking cast and a few more before they would cut it off and I could begin to gingerly walk again. Luckily, all happened in the summer, so I didn't miss any school, but it didn't help Dad with any of the farm work. Oh, I lucked out in one way, the Ford incredibly just needed a little work on the front axle, bending the tie rods back. Dad did say, "That fifty dollars is coming out of your wages, Mick. And you're going to have to convince me I can trust you to get on the tractor again." If ever there was one thing in our Catholic family that was more important, I don't know what it was. Trust was tied into that business of not lying, for damned sure a big sin. And worse, you had to be able to look someone in the eye, in this case Mom and Dad, and see if there was trust in them. Never again did I fool around on the tractor and would be careful to a fault to try not to break anything, including my bones.

I had another bad time with the tractor when doing field work for Dad. This time it wasn't my fault. It was early in the morning and I was getting ready to start the tractor and go out to the field. When I pushed the starter button, flames started up in front of me, on the hood, near the gas tank cover. I turned off the engine, jumped off the tractor and grabbed a gunny sack and tried to beat out the flames. For whatever reason, or the ole' Guardian Angel again, the flames died out. I walked back to the farmhouse, and Mom said, "Mick what are you doing here? You're supposed to be out in the field." "Uh, Mom, there was a small fire near the gas tank. It's out now." For whatever reason, maybe too much else on her mind, Mom just said, "Well, be careful." After a while I went back out, scraped all the grease and soil accumulation near and around the gas tank and cover, started the engine and went on my merry way to the field work. Strange enough, I don't ever remember talking to Dad about it. A good thing I guess.

People say it's pretty boring to grow up and live on a farm. I'm not so sure.

19

SEAN'S STORY – PART II

It must have been one of those icy days in the middle of winter, after supper and the nightly news on the radio when I cornered Dad again, saying "You never finished telling me about those early days and how we got to the farm here. All I remember is you were talking about some Ryans up in Nebraska." He had finished the Kansas City Star paper and must have had some time before bedtime and told me more of his story.

"Mick, we lived on the north bank of the south fork of the Nemeha River in Southeast Nebraska. The house itself was thirty to forty feet from the riverbank. I was standing on the edge of the riverbank and talking to a man across the river and that the very next day that portion of the bank had dropped in. Oh, I forgot, we had an old Quackenbush rifle which shot bullets with shot. We would shoot rats at night in the kitchen!

"I was eleven years old when Dad died and when we moved down to Kansas. I grew up with an old yellow shepherd pup called 'Don.' We kids would take the dog out and get from five to ten rabbits at a time for eating. The method was for us kids to jump up and down on a brush pile and scare out the rabbits which ole' Don would then run down. He went with us on the trip to Kansas and eventually became deaf and blind and died at about eighteen or nineteen years of age.

"Up home on the original homestead in Kansas, Uncle Tim's place now while you are growing up, there was a cistern with a wooden cover which was left open. The same dog jumped in and I pulled it out with a rope, the dog barking the whole time. A good watchdog, he said. It seems that my sister Laura fell into the same cistern when she was a baby. My sister Ann jumped in and pulled her out.

"Whoops, I got ahead of myself. Back in Nebraska we lived on three separate farms. The school district was given land to support itself, and my aunt who was a domestic owned some of this land. My Dad rented the place from her. I was born in 1893. It was the spring of 1898 when we all moved to a second farm, this one north of Dawson, Nebraska. We lived there for two years. This farm was rented from a certain Mr. Ryan. Later on we would move to the south fork of the Nemeha to a farm of one hundred and fifty acres."

Dad was smiling and you could tell he enjoyed all the reminiscing. "We used horses to farm, Cleveland Bays, about 1300 pounds each. The mare was called "Grey Bird" and another called "Black Bird." We got twelve colts from Grey Bird and brought her to Kansas. I was eleven when we came to Kansas. We also had milk cows, a few hogs, chickens and raised wheat and corn. There were four work horses and they always had colts each year. Each horse was worth from one hundred to one hundred and thirty dollars. The stallion was called "Charley," a deep bay.

"My sisters Megan and Lizzie and I were all born on my aunt's place up in Nebraska. Ann and Matthew on the two-year farm in 1898. The landlord of the second farm, Mr. Ryan, had a drugstore in Dawson.

"At that time the house was wood frame. Rural free delivery went in at about that time, coming out of Dawson. We had no phone, but there were a few in the county. About one of ten to fifteen families had a phone. When my Dad died, I rode on horseback to a neighbor's house to call the doctor, this during a cold February. When the snowstorms were bad, you could walk over the fence rows.

"We also had brood sows and turkeys. We generally had about fifty turkeys in the Fall. We would keep from eight to twelve hens and a gobbler. The hens would hide their nests from people, but in the fall the hen would come in with six to ten little ones. The turkeys would fly up into the trees and roost at night. There was a haystack in a meadow, and we would drive the turkeys from the stack, and they would then fly into the barnyard. We would put feed in the granary, the turkeys would come in to eat, and then we would shut the door and catch them. We had a grain wagon with a big box. We would put slats on it and haul the turkeys to town that way. We got eleven to fourteen cents a pound. Also sold chicken eggs in town, at three cents a dozen."

Dad really got tickled here; he could hardly talk when he told this story. "There was a fat lady in the neighborhood who must have weighed about three hundred pounds, name was Lola. Had a sister named Maud who probably weighed about two hundred pounds. They came over and wanted to buy a turkey, and Dad sold them a year-old gobbler that weighed twenty-six pounds. Lola had a horse and buggy. She sold picture frames and delivered them over the county. Somehow or other Dad was always trying to get Lola to tell how much she weighed or find it out. He got her to drive the buggy up on a scale, supposedly to weigh the turkey. She would never get up on the scale but would always walk around it. One time Lola came to see us and cracked a board on the front porch and fell through it and fainted." (Dad heehawed here.)

"Dad smoked a pipe and had a white, bushy beard. He was forty-three years old when he died of cancer of the stomach or ulcers. He was never a well man. They tried three times to build him up so they could operate on him. He left insurance money, and it was with that that Mom bought the land in Kansas at Buckeye northeast of Abilene. She brought originally eighty acres with a small house for $2,800. All that's a long story; I've got to get to bed and so do you. Maybe we can continue this another night."

20

WHEAT HARVEST – MICK HELPING OUT

Dad must have been talking about farm work the next morning, and now that I was older, I would get my share of it. Paul was working in a nearby town as an estimator for a small company that manufactured elevators or lifts for farm buildings; Joe and I were left to do a lot of the farm work. First comes to my mind the most important, wheat harvest.

Wheat harvest time was important, an event much anticipated, with joy when a bumper crop was expected, with sadness when the wheat was thin. In the 1940s and 50s only the very prosperous farmers had their own big, self-propelled combines; the small family farms still used the old pull-type combines in some cases, but more than likely hired the professional harvest crews on a share basis. These latter were medium to big operations, generally consisting in two or three or more large self-propelled models like Massey Harris, John Deere, or International Harvester. Also, the crews had to have several large grain trucks. The combines sometimes were driven along the country highways at about 25 to 30 miles per hour, but for long distances were transported on the same large grain trucks. Living quarters in the early 50s was generally a modified school bus with bunks. Cooking facilities were at a minimum also since main meals were prepared by the farmer's wife or were taken in small country cafes in the neighboring towns. Local farm kids often joined a crew and worked from June through early August on the route which started in Texas or Oklahoma, worked its way through central and western Kansas, on up into Nebraska, eastern Colorado and perhaps Wyoming or the Dakotas.

I never worked with the custom cutters, primarily because I was needed by Dad to help with the local farm work all summer long. I can recall Dad using an old yellow pull-type combine for a while, maybe a Massey-Harris, but it was not reliable, constantly under repair, and Dad with the frustration of it all relented to hire a professional crew, but at a high cost. I can remember some of the breakdowns, a frustrating and nervous time, eventually not to be tolerated. The wheat was ripe, and it was also rain, hail, and tornado season. An entire crop in the field could be obliterated or at least partially ruined with much lower yield with additional rain that would cause the wheat to lie down and not be high enough for the combine pickup to get it.

Time was of the essence, thus harvest crews worked long days. Starting time was dictated by humidity and moisture content in the wheat; the grain elevator would take wheat only with low moisture content and penalize the farmer at a certain point. If you began to cut too early in the day, you could lose out. Once the drying started, however, cutting went on into the late hours of the night, sometimes all night long. The crews had a reputation for some raucous living; supposedly a lot of beer drinking and womanizing went on after hours, or on the rainy days when work was impossible, although I think a lot more sitting around waiting or work repairing machinery was more likely.

Luke Zimmerman's cousins from Thomas, Oklahoma, ran such a crew, a sad story for me one year. One of the crew, a big tough Oklahoma farmer-football player had a short flirtation with a local girl I had been dating. (That's high school, more on that later.) There wasn't much I could do about it, and it turned out for the best, but I didn't think so at the time. It hurt way down deep.

I believe the harvesters would charge according to the acre, so many dollars per acre. The local farmer's net depended on how many bushels he got to the acre and the price of wheat. There were times when he did not make much, but in the case of the small farmer there was little choice. Dad could not afford to buy a big combine himself, and the old, worn out pull model just did not get the job done. But, in general harvest was a happy time, a lot of hard work to be sure, but the big pay day of the year in Kansas. I can recall the thrill of riding up on the combine while they cut; I never did drive one since I was too young when Dad combined and later on the custom crews handled it.

One of my jobs during Dad's days was to drive the trailer under the combine chute to empty the grain into the trailer for hauling to town. You could drive at age 14 in Kansas if you lived on a farm, so between the tractor and all you learned in a hurry. There was constant talk of wheat prices, about a dollar a bushel in bad times when Dad farmed in the 50s. Dad cut his own wheat or traded off with a neighbor who had a combine. I generally helped by driving the grain trailer hitched to our old car to the grain elevator in town where there were always long lines waiting to dump the wheat. When I was very tiny, I used to ride along with Dad or Mom when they hauled the wheat to town in a trailer pulled by the car or a borrowed truck, a small but workable arrangement. I was always scared when they lifted the truck or trailer up on the hoist to dump the wheat and was also a bit pensive thinking what would happen if you fell into the pit. Stories abounded about deaths in the grain elevators, generally when moving grain or the like, sometimes an explosion or sometimes by poisonous air.

But the trip into town was fun for a country boy. First of all, you got a change of scene from the farm and got to talk to people, and I generally got a bottle of pop or a pop cycle when I went along for the ride. I can recall the long waits at the railroad tracks while all the switching of cars took place. There were three railroads through Abilene in those days, the Union Pacific, the Rock Island and the Santa Fe. The grain elevators were located by the tracks since all grain was eventually transported by rail. The elevators had to empty storage space for harvest of the new crop, and the wheat was transferred to Kansas City. There was a constant switching process going on; it seemed like that should all have been done ahead of time, long before harvest, but it never seemed to work out that way.

Oftentimes it was dry, hot, perfect weather for harvest. But sometimes there was rain and the combines would get stuck in the fields. The crews began to use huge tires, "airplane tires" (the huge inner tubes were a mainstay at the local swimming pool where we played "king of the mountain" on them for years), to get through the mud in the fields. This of course left the fields in an incredible mess when they dried and made the plowing a lot tougher later on.

21

TIME TO PLOW

Of course, after harvest, it was time to plow. I helped Dad with the fieldwork for many summers. There never was an exact wage scale; I think our system was that he gave me an allowance for incidentals, but that the wages were to go into an account to pay for college. Back to the plowing. It was still accepted practice to totally turn the soil under, the idea being to return the straw, etc. to the soil for mulch. That meant plowing. All those years we used our tiny Ford tractor with a two-bottom plow, turning over maybe a two-foot width of soil each round. I can't remember well, but I think it did an acre an hour. The years varied greatly, not only with the amount of wheat harvested, but the kind of stubble or growth left after cutting: some years, stubble was so thick and damp it was almost impossible to turn under. So we often would disk the field first to break up the stubble, and then plow. I remember that one of the most disagreeable parts of that job was the plow getting all jammed up with the stubble and I would have to stop the tractor, get off and manually pull the stubble out. Time after time after time.

So we would disk, plow, disk later to break up the big clods and eventually harrow until the field was a soft, fine consistency. All this was to prepare the soil for planting that fall. I can't believe the number of times we went over the same ground. And like everything else, there was a fine line between preparing the soil properly and not. If it was too fine and you got strong winds, always a possibility in Kansas, it would blow, and the irreplaceable topsoil would head off toward Missouri and eventually end up as silt in the Mississippi. There were times when it would start to blow and we would rush to the field to disk, thus breaking the surface into clods and bringing a bit of moisture to the surface. Weather was always a primary subject on the farm, and although we had the rain gage, Dad was uncanny after a rain, estimating the amount closely. He also seemed to know how much moisture was in the soil, even when it appeared totally dry on top.

Given my 'iff ens, I probably would have preferred a nice job in town to the farm work. Much of it was boring to me, and I regret to this day not "applying myself," working harder and "doing it right." But Dad had little choice; if he wanted the help, he had to accept my less than perfect work patterns. It wasn't that I was lazy, but rather I just sometimes didn't get the hang of it. I used to get bored silly out on that tractor, and some of the antics I pulled must have appalled him. For starters, I would sing or whistle every song I had ever heard on the radio, sing until my throat got too sore, and then whistle. I used to pride myself on my whistling, like the theme from the "High and the Mighty" a great adventure airline pilot film with John Wayne. If I'm no expert now, it certainly is not for a lack of practice time then.

I sang pop songs, country songs, church songs and whistled classic melodies, overtures to Operas from brother Paul's record collection, show tunes and the like. "South Pacific" and "Carousel" were from that period.

When plowing, for those of you blessed with no knowledge of it, the right tractor wheels are in the furrow, inclined slightly, so only a little pressure on the steering wheel was necessary. I used to close my eyes and see how far and long I could go without opening my eyes and/or getting out of the furrow. It even got to the point sometimes when I would intentionally try to fall asleep for brief moments until I would wake up and find myself, tractor and plow heading off down the middle of the field, out of the furrow. It only happened a time or two, but it demonstrates my keen concentration and state of mind at the time. I guess I was a scamp at times, and there are many times to tell.

Now, if it rained enough, it got too muddy to plow. I was the quickest "tractor" west of the Mississippi to get back to the house when there was scarcely a sprinkle. I recall once or twice when they sent me back out to the field. You get mighty thirsty out in that sun, heat and dirt. I carried ice water in a jug that most farmers would carry on the tractor. Not me. I would leave it in a place where there was at least a little shade under a solitary tree or some tall brome grass. That meant stopping the tractor ever so often for a drink. Sometimes it was the only way I could manage to make another long round around the field.

What I really liked was plowing down by the highway; I knew most of the local cars and would wave at each when I made a round near the highway. There was a cute girl in my class at school who lived just down the highway, and when their old 49' Chevy went by, it would brighten my day. I doubt that she ever realized that, but on the other hand, oftentimes her mother would be along with her.

Another diversion, such as it was, in plowing as you leave a smaller and smaller plot of ground toward the center of the field, all the tiny wildlife retreats to the center or the unplowed section. As you finished a given field there was considerable to see: small field mice, ground squirrels, and hawks circling to dive for the rodents.

Eventually I covered all our arable land. Over the course of several years, working for neighbors and friends, I figure I farmed a few thousand acres in Dickinson County which kind of gave me a nice feeling to dream in some way that it was mine and that I had dominion over it. I farmed north, northeast, southeast, south, southwest and northwest of Abilene one time or another. I plowed, disked, cultivated corn, harrowed, and helped bale hay, fill silo, most of the really unskilled work that was needed in those parts. Early on, wages were one dollar an hour and eventually in my time went up to about a dollar and a half. It made spending money during the summer and a little bit toward clothes for school.

22

THE GREAT ENTERPRISE BANK ROBBERY

It was during one of those plowing days when something damned scary happened. I was told later it was what the local papers called "The Great Enterprise Bank Robbery." Enterprise is a tiny town some five miles east of Abilene along the Smokey Hill River. It must have had maybe 500 people in those days, with a tiny business district. I found out only later that some local bank robbers made a heist one hot summer day, and fled toward Abilene, heading in the general direction of our half-section.

I was doing my normal thing, singing songs to keep from going to sleep, plowing down toward Highway 40. I could hear sirens down the highway east and suddenly this old sedan careened around the corner from the highway and up the road on the east side of the farm. It screeched to a stop and a guy jumped out and came running at me on the tractor. I didn't know what in the hell was going on, but he ran closer and I saw he had a gun in his hand and was yelling, "Get the hell off that tractor!" Scared shitless, I stopped, got off and who knows, maybe from seeing too many old cowboy movies put my hands in the air. He grabbed me, forced my hands behind my back and moved us back to the car. "Shut up sonny, don't make a move or it will be curtains for you." Now there were police cars tearing up the county road heading toward us. He fired a shot in the air out the window and shouted, "Don't come any closer or the kid gets it." His cohort was in the driver's seat and he had me in the back seat with the gun pointing at me and a hand around my neck.

All of a sudden there were more police cars, highway patrol and even an airplane or two in the air above us. The guy in the front seat bent over, pulled a "tommy gun" from the right side, opened the door, and faced the first cops, yelling "We got the kid in here and we mean business." Hell, I'm only twelve, too young to die, a skinny guy and shaking in my boots. The guy holding me, yanked me out of the back seat, still holding my neck, me in front of him, I guess so the police would believe him, pointing a gun at my head and said, "Don't come any closer or he gets it. Clear out and give us a head start. The kid goes with us."

What happened next was a blur, and a lot out of character. In an impulsive move, not thinking on my part, I got an arm loose and swinging it down like an ax to cut off a chicken's head, managed to knock the guy's gun arm down and dove for the ditch at the side of the road. There were blasts of guns on all sides. The police had unloaded their shotguns and pistols on my captor, blasting him and the driver while I was on the ground trying to crawl away from the car. It was like Bonny and Clyde and the shootout with the feds. One of the police came up and said, "You are one lucky son of a bitch, but a brave one. Are you hurt?"

I was bruised and sore but, Jesus, no wounds, just shaking in my boots and my jeans all wet. Christ, I had peed my pants in the melee. "I guess not. But I don't feel so good." That was when I threw up in front of him. So with wet pants and throw up all over me, they picked me up, moved me in the back of the police car and said, "We're hustling you into the hospital kid." "What about the tractor?" (I must have been in shock.) "Boy, that's the least of your worries. I think you'll get a medal to put on the steering wheel."

All I remember is one very fast ride up to the hospital, just a mile or two down the road, being rushed into a room which seemed all white, with white sheets on a bed, and a nurse giving me some kind of a shot. I woke up a few hours later, everything groggy and fuzzy with Dad, Mom, Paul, Caitlin and Joe all in the room. I guess I was in shock or some such thing, but they brought me warm soup and then some ice cream. I recounted all I could remember. Dear Mom had her rosary in her hand, came and hugged me, and said, "Enough excitement for one day, Mick. Your guardian angel must have been on the back of the tractor." Dad said, "You get the rest of the day off; I'll go get the tractor. But you're not off the hook. Maybe you can go back out tomorrow or the next day. That south 80 isn't finished yet."

The event made the local paper the next day, "Farm Boy Foils Bank Robbers," and I became a celebrity for a few days. We used to think, all of us, that not much ever happened on the farm in those days. Evidently, not so.

23

HAY AND CORN, WORK AND MISCHIEF

In a few days I did get back to the plowing, but Dad had more in store. Hay baling was another of the big jobs in summer. In that part of Kansas, we could cut three or perhaps four hay crops each summer, all depending on the weather. Each cutting was a bit less than the previous as summer went along. A vague, hazy memory is that of an old-fashioned threshing machine, not a steam thresher, but a gasoline-driven thresher driven by a belt from an old "Johnny Popper" or old time John Deere tractor with a pulley that drove the belt. This was for alfalfa seed harvesting. The residual, or the hay itself, came out loose and was stacked by hand using pitchforks. I am sure I did witness that as a very young boy.

But the more normal way was of course to mow the hay, rake it into windrows, then bale with a semi-automatic baler. I worked for one neighbor down by the river on one of the old block and tie jobs where the crew in the field was four: one man on the tractor, two on the baler, one to tie the baling wire around the bale, the other to block or section each bale, and a fourth on the hayrack pulled behind the baler. It was all hot, dirty and sweaty, but particularly so on the baler. I was a hired hand in this case, but Dad also used the old block and tie baler in the earlier days. It was borrowed, traded or leased, one farmer who owned the baler doing the work in exchange for help on his own hay or fieldwork.

Hay baling makes me think of the old barn dances of those days. They were big affairs held at night in the haymow or barn of a local farmer and were a cause for a gathering of many, many local folks. There may have been a square dance caller, perhaps with a little record player and p.a. system, but there were at least a few times when we had a real "live" band: fiddle, guitar or two, maybe a banjo, drums. I was too tiny to dance but enjoyed the milling around and camaraderie with other buddies, all of us too young for girls at the time.

Back to the hay. Later on came the automatic baler that did the tying and blocking automatically, thus eliminating two men from the crew. But even then it seemed the bailers were constantly jamming, breaking the wires or something. Even with the new balers you still needed quite a crew: one group in the field baling, one or two driving the tractor and hauling the hayracks between the field and the barn, and a crew up in the barn stacking the bales as they came in. That's where our old-fashioned barn and haymow came in.

The barn seemed to be to be a huge old place, two stories high with the hayloft up above with an inclined driveway to a big open door so you could drive a small tractor and hayrack inside, a smaller door on the opposite end for ventilation, and a few windows on the sides. I worked several of those summers up there; the sweet smell of the hay, but the incredible heat and humidity, the flies and the sweat. We did not have fans, so the only ventilation was an occasional breeze, such as it was. But I remember a lot of small talk, banter, joking, laughing and good times during those days. Joe seemed to be in the middle of it. As usual there was a scary part for a kid: after the hayrack was empty, someone had to grab the tongue of the rack, all would give a push, and it gradually gained speed, seeming to zoom down the incline and in between the silo and the granary before coming to a stop and then being hitched to the little Ford tractor for another run to the field. Paul must have got off work to help because I remember him hanging on to the tongue and running the rack down the hill between the silo and the granary. I think I eventually could handle that part, but only when I was older. It's funny how things like that, so seemingly minute and unimportant, really marked one's growing up. Joe would help for a while either on the hayrack or the barn, but his really bad hay fever put an end to that. Not me, no hay fever.

One last memory was the arrival each summer of the big semi hay trucks from Texas that would buy a good part of that year's crop, and for $1.00 per bale.

Dad did all our hay mowing with the little Ford and sometimes I would rake. I had trouble making the windrows straight enough and botched up the corners, still easier said than done to do a good job, but I worked mainly on the hay rack or in the barn. I have always thought there was a big difference between the Irish and German immigrant farmers around Abilene. I still think the Irish all in all did it right (they had more fun but made less money). Our bales were lighter by quite a few pounds, easier to handle, and we took it a bit easier. Dad would work on Sunday only out of absolute necessity, like during wheat harvest. He always took Sunday off whenever possible, and I am convinced it saved his sanity and also added years to his life. (Sunday afternoon was when he would disappear to the Elks Club to play pitch or gin rummy with the locals, several who were lawyers, doctors, and businessmen. They were no match for his card playing memory and I recall he would often come home with what he called "grocery money" from the card games.) There were German farmers south of town (river bottom land, the best around) I worked for at times; I could barely lift their bales. They were larger, more efficient, more hay in them, and greener sometimes. The green hay reminds me of barn fires. We never had one, but they were not all that uncommon. If the hay was too wet when baled and was stacked tightly in the barn, sometimes the process of spontaneous combustion could start a spark, and the whole crop and barn would burn down. There was one German south of town that we always marveled at, how he never managed to have a fire since he always was in a big hurry to bale. Since then I have realized that most of the German farmers worked the same way. I do recall seeing a humongous barn fire near Enterprise when I was very little, and wet hay was the cause. There were huge flames in the night sky and no rural fire department to take care of it.

But one of the joys of being a small boy or even a teenager on the farm was that during slack times during the summer or later on in the year I would have buddies over to play, and inevitably we would build hay forts in the barn. I remember Doug Eagleton in particular. We had tunnels, forts with windows, etc. and used two tin cans with a taut string between them for a walkie-talkie (remember I read comic books and Blackhawk and GI Joe that were still big, Korean War days). Most of the time it was friends from town that came out, because buddies who lived on farms had enough of it already and preferred to play sports. That barn played a big role in my growing up. But that's another story. Little Jimmie Dickens had a song "Out behind the barn," and with some truth to it.

During all this time Paul was not around much; he was 15 years older than I and was already working as an estimator and then salesman at Ehrsams' Manufacturing Company in Enterprise. Joe had a horrible case of hay fever and although he did some work on the farm in earlier years, he flew the coop by getting a job at the State 4-H Camp near Rock Springs, a few miles from Abilene, a place where I think he had a chance to become quite a ladies' man and also where he sunburned his body a few too many times as a lifeguard. I always envied that job: great food, meeting all the girls, horseback riding and swimming, and fun nights carousing.

But I had nary a bit of hay fever, don't think I got stuffed up or even sneezed much. Destiny.

But there's a story about Joe when he still worked on the farm. During one of the hay baling times he was introduced to chewing tobacco, once again by my old friend of the 12-gauge shotgun days, cousin Elfred. (Elfred had taught me how to shoot the gun with the recoil knocking me to the ground and giving me a black and blue face the next day.) I recall Joe coming in from the field at noon for the big farm meal for all the workers, and he could handle a big plate loaded up with fried chicken, mounds of mashed potatoes, tomatoes, heaping the plate high. Suddenly Tom grew quiet and then "blam!" headed for the bathroom. We laughed and laughed. For that reason and who knows what else I never tried chewing tobacco or snuff. Dad once said that when he was twenty - two, fresh out of the Merchant Marine during World War I days, he smoked cigarettes, pipe and chewed, all during the same years. Later he went cold turkey, gave it all up and never smoked again. I never saw him use tobacco.

Back to the field work. Another mainstay on the farm, when there was sufficient rain and a good year, was corn. The "South Pacific" song "I'm as corny as Kansas in August" is a misnomer, at least as dry land farming in Central Kansas goes (try Nebraska or Iowa). There was no way we could grow a good corn crop without an unusually wet year, and those were few and far between. I recall many years when the corn would begin to dry up, a decision was made to cut it all up for ensilage, at least that way, salvaging some of the crop. But there were good years too.

I can recall one very disagreeable job in those times: after corn gets to a certain height, it is no longer possible to run a cultivator through it without knocking down the corn. So there was only one way: Dad, Joe and I would walk the field row by row with hoes to cut out sunflowers and cockle burrs. That was when Joe's hay fever acted up most, he was truly miserable.

I also remember that in those days Dad kept a lot of hogs and fed them field corn; my job was to drive the tractor pulling the trailer, the same one we hauled wheat in July, but now with a sideboard attached. Dad and Joe too I think would walk alongside the wagon with shucking gloves on, a leather glove with a metal protrusion, much like the end of a beer opener. They would shuck the corn, that is, pick it and throw the ear against the sideboard and bounce it into the wagon. I eventually did some shucking myself but was not too handy at it. Dad talked of the old days and shucking contests back in Nebraska. He was fast and good. I can remember bringing the corn to the storage bins in the hog house and having a machine that would shell it and put it into the bin. We fed bushels and bushels to the hogs in those days, and to the cattle too. That was what we used to call real "corn fed" livestock.

The actual corn picking or harvesting was done by a neighbor who had a corn picker or harvester. We never had one. It was common in those days to hear about farmers who had horrendous accidents - the corn picker would jam, they would not turn it off, would stick a hand or an arm in to pull out the jammed stocks, the machine would unclog, and the farmer's arm or hand would get caught by the sleeve. We had three or four one-armed or one-handed farmers in the town. I had great fear and respect instilled in me about machines, and we never had a serious accident on our farm (from machinery that is; there were plenty of others.)

It seemed like we would plant milo or sorghum more than corn, and I am not exactly sure why, because all the row crops needed copious amounts of rain. But Dad was very up to date in his crop rotation techniques and also the care of the land. Mom often spoke of what terrible shape the farm was in 1941 when Dad got it and how he improved it by terracing, contour farming (planting along the sides of the terraces instead of perpendicular to them, up and down the hills, thus saving moisture and preventing soil erosion). I recall we would go through a cycle of wheat or corn, then alfalfa which would put nitrogen back into the soil. My Dad's proudest and finest achievement was with waterways allowing proper run off, good terracing, planting of windbreaks and creating what we called "the pond" at the north end of the farm, an eroded area he turned into a lush haven for birds, squirrels and an abundance of black walnut producing trees. It was all done through good management. I am not sure where he learned all that, but I know he subscribed to farm journals and kept in close contact with county farm extension people. You figure, he lived on a farm his entire life, from the time in SE Nebraska.

I was always very proud of our farm and the way Dad ran it, how it looked, even though we did not have the resources others did. He had a balance in farming and in life that many did not have. He worked to the best of his abilities, but managed to enjoy life along the way, something I did not see in many of the families we knew.

24

FEARS FOR DAD AND MOM

There were times when I was terrified for Dad, not in a way that I would wonder "What's to become of us if something happens to him?" but simply for his physical safety. One such time dealt with the Ford tractor.

The little Ford tractor was versatile, and there was a way to switch the very heavy back tires around for a wider space between them for working row crops-cultivating corn, weeding milo, and the like. But the process was arduous, tricky and dangerous. It involved setting up a sort of jack under the rear axle, using the hydraulic system and the power takeoff to lift up the entire rear part of the tractor resulting in the big heavy rear wheels being left off the ground. Dad would have to loosen and take off all the big bolts on the tire and then manhandle the big tire loose, slowly turn it around and put it back on the tractor in the new position. It was a job involving two people, one person to sit on the tractor seat and run the control for the power takeoff, the other to move the wheel. So, I helped Dad many times and was scared to death for him. One time there was an especially close call. He loosened the bolts and told me, "Grab the power takeoff lever and move it up." The rear end of the tractor slowly lifted off the ground and the big wheel was revolving free. I can recall what seemed to me as quiet desperation and effort that it took to move the tire, Dad's face and upper body totally bathed in sweat through a blue work shirt, how he had to move so slowly and carefully or the tire could go toppling off in the opposite direction to the ground, or worse yet, falling on him to break a leg or worse. He managed to get the tire off, roll it around and place it back on the rim so to match the big threaded bolts with the nuts. Finally he said, "Lower the power takeoff lever." I did, and the rear end plus wheel sunk to the ground. So that time the tire never fell; but there were close calls.

There were times like that when I saw Dad try to fix equipment, mend things and I realized the struggle it was to keep things going. It is very, very difficult to explain, but when I had to help him with something mechanical, I would almost get sick to my stomach, such was the aversion I had to things mechanical. I guess that explains my total lack of mechanical aptitude as I write this yet now. (People talk of right-side and left side of the brain; I still don't get it, but something has to explain the way I am.) I can remember a time or two with the tiny Ford tractor torn completely apart up in the haymow, some kind of an overhaul operation, I think. There was no alternative for Dad - either do the work himself, or at least most of it, or quit farming. The thing was, he never had a particularly mechanical aptitude himself; I think it was pure necessity that made him keep going.

Another time I had serious fears for Dad's safety that sticks in my mind was during the drought years when our well seemed to fail; that, or the pump at the bottom stopped. Whichever, it meant that Dad had to tie one end of a long rope to a tree, wrap the other end around his waist, and lower himself down into the dark, damp hole. I guess it was approximately 40 to 50 feet down, but it seemed like half-way to China to me. I would watch him lower himself ever so carefully over the edge and on down. This time as he was lowering himself, for some reason and I don't know how, the knot of the rope around the tree came loose. I think Dad was about halfway down to the bottom. He yelled, "Mick, I'm falling and can't stop the fall. Grab the rope and hang on." The sides of the well hole were basically lined with rock and concrete and Dad tried to break the fall with his feet. I think he had work shoes on. It wasn't enough.

For whatever reason, I didn't have gloves on, either the leather ones we used for baling hay or even cotton for gardening. There was no time to think. I grabbed the rope with my bare hands, fell to the ground, braced my feet against the concrete-stone ring around the well hole and held on. I was still a skinny runt then and not very strong at that, but at least managed to slow Dad's fall. I heard a loud thud and splash when he hit bottom, groaned and in his not usual voice, managed to yell up at me. "Mick, good job. I'm all banged up and my feet, ankles and knees hurt, damn, and my arms and shoulders too. But I'm only in about a foot of water." I wasn't in such good shape myself, both of my hands bloodied from the rope. And I think I was crying. Dad yelled from the bottom, "Mick there's another rope hanging up down in the cellar. Go get it, hang on to one end and drop the other down to me. I'll tie it to this one, you can pull as much as you need and wrap the damned thing around that tree several times, and tie and knot it three or four times. Test it and let me know when you're done."

I ran down the steps into the cellar, turned on that light up on the ceiling, and couldn't see any rope. I panicked but somehow saw in one of the dark corners the coil of rope. I grabbed it, both my hands in agony, ran back out to the well. Mom was there by now and had heard all the commotion. She said, "Be careful. Sean, are you hurt?" Dad yelled up, "Molly I'm okay, just banged up. Check on Mick and see if he's getting that rope tied okay." I did and she checked, after a bit Dad pulled it taut and started to climb up out of the well. He had to stop and rest several times. There was no way we could grab on and help him or he might have taken another tumble. I was never so happy in my life when I saw his face, shoulders and arms, finally his waist, legs and feet crawl over the side of the well. He has scrapes all over his arm and his face and was sweating from the effort. He said, "You'll have to do without water today. I'll go back down tomorrow and fix the pump. Right now if you don't mind, I'm going to get some 'medicine.' Molly, get the bourbon bottle up on the shelf in the hall closet and pour me a juice glass full." Dad never but never overdid it on the booze, was not a daily or even weekly drinker, but on special occasions, I guess. This sure as hell was one! The bottle was a pint of Old

Grandad. In this case Mom never hesitated and as Dad sat on the concrete steps of the old windmill by the well hole, he took a couple of swigs, winced, smiled at us and said, "I reckon St. Christopher or someone was helping us on this deal. Mick, slowing that fall maybe saved me some broken bones or worse. Molly get him a big RC Cola; he deserves it. And help him wash and soak his hands and get bandaged up."

This wasn't the first or only time such things happened or could have happened. Mom went to the medicine cabinet in the bathroom, grabbed the cotton, gauze and tape, took me into the sink, ran cold water on the bloody hands, put mercurochrome on the rope burns and taped me up. Then she pulled a big RC Cola out of the fridge, and said, "If you want another one, this might be the time."

The feeling of relief was overpowering when Dad came into the house a bit later. I think he took the rest of that day off, saying, "Mick, you're doing all the chores tonight." The next morning, he redid the rope, checking the knot a couple of extra times, lowered himself down again. I heard some banging on the pipes or the metal pump. I do not remember yet the problem at that specific time, if we needed a new pump or what, but it got fixed. And once again, the relief when he climbed out of that hole was overwhelming.

With Mom I can remember a couple of accidents. One time a Coca Cola bottle exploded when she opened the icebox door, cutting her severely on the shins and legs. But a scarier time was when she choked on a fishbone at supper one night. It seemed like it all was in slow motion - she coughed and coughed, gagged, turned red and I was scared to death. It turned out all right but put a healthy respect for fish bones in my mind to the present.

25

DAD'S STORY – PART III – THE MOVE TO KANSAS AND THE FARM

On another of those evenings on the farm, I corralled Dad after supper to continue his tales of growing up, Nebraska, and then the move to Kansas. This time we were all out on the front porch, Dad sitting in a rocking chair and Joe, Caitlin and me on the wood steps. Mom was in a straight back chair on the east side of the porch, working on yet another of the rag rugs she painstakingly wove and used on the hard wood floors of the dining and living room.

"Mick, Joe and Caitlin, the family moved down to Kansas in an immigrant car (a box car) loaded at Dawson, Nebraska, in the spring of 1906. We took three horses, one cow and machinery, a binder and a plow. We went to Sabetha where we all got on a passenger train. Mom had a food basket. We took the train from there to Marysville. Then we got on a 'hog train' to Manhattan, this train having one passenger car. There we changed to the Union Pacific to get as far as Detroit, Kansas, five miles east of Abilene. My brother Liam met the train with five or six teams and wagons to haul the machinery out to the homestead. We all then went up to the new farm in a spring wagon, a carriage without a top, pulled by two horses.

The old house on the homestead farm at Buckeye had three rooms aside from the kitchen: one room upstairs where the women slept, one down where the men slept, and a dining room. We had a wood stove and burned hedge wood which had to be enclosed because it sparked. We used corn cobs for kindling to start the stove. It heated the dining room and kitchen. Everybody slept on feather tick (goose down) with straw tick or clean corn husks under that. There were no mattresses. That reminds me: in my grandad's house in Nebraska we would awaken with snow on the blankets in the morning. You had to have bedclothes."

Mom interjected here that she lived in a sod house when teaching in eastern Colorado.

Dad went on, "Eight years later, with the money from milk cows, we bought the eighty acres south of the original place on Buckeye. We had had six head of red shorthorns to start out. And we had hogs, a couple of sows. Generally we had calves to sell. We would bucket feed them and in the Fall they would weigh from four hundred to five hundred pounds and would sell for sixty to seventy dollars apiece.

I perked up at that point, "Hey Dad I've seen you do that out the door in front of the milk house of the barn. I had no idea exactly why or where that all came from, but now I see you had a plan."

"Mick, there's always a plan. Back to the old farm north of Buckeye. The new eighty-acres were bought for about $3,000. Mom borrowed money from the bank to do it. My brother Liam bought a third eighty next to the second. We raised horses, as many as thirty head at a time. Had two six-horse teams. Rented the quarter of land across the road to the east, this in 1913. Now there was a total of four 80s in all. In 1918 when World War I broke out, we had three six-horse teams. The boys worked for shares, not wages. At this time Tim another of my brothers, bought the first mules for the farm; they were tougher and worked better than the horses. Back in 1917 I had started to do some farming for himself, thirty acres of corn."

After returning from the service, the Merchant Marine, in 1918 (Dad used to tell stories of sleeping in hammocks in the ship, of a time when he was on lookout up in the crow's nest and during a storm it was almost horizontal to the water), Dad and others helped build a new house on the original eighty, the one that we all knew as Tim and Martha's while growing up in the 1940s and 1950s. Dad moved at this time and rented the Roupe place, a farm about one mile east of the one I grew up on, located a few miles south of the old homestead on old Highway 40 and lived on it until 1925.

26

SEAN – HIGH ADVENTURE OUT WEST – THE MOTORCYCLE DIARY

The motorcycle trip out West in 1925. This is the story Dad would tell so often, and Mom would just get up and go into the other room because she had heard it so often and knew it by memory by now. Dad picked fruit, helped a truck farmer outside of Denver, worked at a huge dairy in Oregon and drove a huge team, 36 horses if I am not mistaken, combining wheat in eastern Washington State. As he told these stories, they came to take on an epic tone, and you could tell he loved the freedom of it all, the adventure of being "on the road" in the twenties. But there seemed to be more and more milk cows milked each morning, more and more horses on the combine team as he told and retold.

On the 1925 trip there were no paved roads at all. Somewhere, lost now, I have seen pictures of Dad in a spiffy Irish-type hat, and high laced leather boots, well-polished, at about this time. In the Fall of 1926 Dad arrived back home at the home place. His brothers Tim and Liam had both married and were gone, so Dad ran the farm, the original home place. It consisted of five eighties. They raised some cattle, had Holsteins for milking and sold the calves. They bought Holstein bull calves from the orphanage herd on Highway 15 up north of town and heifer calves at sales.

By 1934, the depression years, they had some 75 to 80 head. They kept 22 calves or yearlings. In 1933 they had hogs, sold about 65 head of fat hogs twice a year. They were sold in Kansas City for $2.85 a hundred, about three cents a pound. Dad said they would raise a hog, sell it, and buy a cow. They sold cattle in 1935 for about $275 a head.

As he told this, Dad had a thought and just started laughing and couldn't stop. He said, "Kansas City. That always makes me think of the church preacher in Abilene who told his church folks that if they put a hog in a railway car down on the Union Pacific and prayed real hard, the hog would multiply to a whole herd by the time the train got to Kansas City. Hee hee hee."

27

MOM (MOLLY'S) STORY – PART I

There was a lot more to our story, Irish-Catholic in Kansas, than Dad's life. Mom's was just as interesting but in a different way. The Ryans meshed well with the O'Briens. I got her side of it about the same way as Dad's, one summer evening when all the dishes were done and we were all on the front porch, enjoying that cool southeast breeze, hearing the bird sounds and the cicadas. Mom was sitting on the porch rocking chair, her apron still on and a wet dish cloth in her lap. I said, "Mom, Dad's told me so much of his story. How about you?"

Mom (I loved her Irish nickname of Molly from Maureen) said, "It's a long story, but you are right; Sean doesn't have much on me." Dad who was in the other rocker, guffawed and said, "Mick, she's right. You won't find a tougher and sweeter Irish farm girl than this."

Mom said, "Where to start? I guess like your Dad did, from the beginning.

"I was born in Solomon, Kansas, in 1900, on a farm one mile west and south of town. The farm had 160 acres. My parents were Michael Ryan and Minnie Callahan Ryan. Michael had been married before, thus I had two half-brothers, Leon and George. My father Michael died of typhoid fever in 1905, so I and my two half-brothers, farmed the land.

"A certain John Donnelly lived just up the road, and Minnie eventually married him, her second marriage, in November of 1908. They then bought a farm near Kipp, Kansas, fifteen miles southwest of Solomon.

(I saw that farmhouse with Mom and Dad while on a drive, some years back.) John and Minnie had no honeymoon trip. I remember spending that time, what might have been honeymoon time, at the old Callahan house in Solomon. My uncle Nick Callahan lived there at the time.

"I went to school in Kipp, Kansas, a one-room country school. We lived by a creek and always went ice skating in the winter. We rode to school in the 'hack,' a wagon with seats and a canvas covering so you could roll it up in nice weather. My chores were to sweep the floor in the house and help clean it on Saturdays. I liked to be outside. (Is this where Mom got her love of birds and passed it all on to us, often looking out the small north window of the kitchen over the sink at the birds?) Another chore was to pick up corncobs and hedge wood for the fire.

I went to school in Kipp until a sophomore in high school, then to Sacred Heart Academy in Salina, Kansas. I boarded in Salina from Monday to Friday and rode the train from Salina to Kipp on weekends, a 22-cent fare. Some friends and I would go to the movies once or twice a week in Salina for ten to fifteen cents. I remember staying with the Sullivans in their boarding house. They were 'misers' and gave me mainly oatmeal and coffee for food. They tried to make me eat the oatmeal with coffee instead of milk. I never really did get enough to eat. Lucky for me a new boarder came in that year, and I was invited to move with her and her daughter to a different boarding house, but now with plenty to eat. I went home on weekends, riding the caboose of freight trains. (I remember all the trains going through Abilene, the Union Pacific, the Santa Fe and even the Rock Island from the North, all with cabooses and a conductor standing in the back.) Later on I boarded with a Mrs. Taylor in Salina. About that time I had a roommate, Eileen Brennan of Hays, who never took a bath, but she was a 'good girl.' We often went to the movies together in 1916-1917.

"During my senior year at Sacred Heart I lived with Mrs. Wilburs on the east side of Iron Avenue in Salina. I walked to school and came home at noon for lunch. I had studied German at Kipp and Latin at Sacred Heart with some tough Catholic nuns. Central and Western Kansas then had lots of Germans along with the Irish. I studied piano all four years; the final recital was a big event. Three girls were playing at the same time at one piano. I graduated 5ᵗʰ in a class of 17. There were no extra-curricular activities in those days.

"But there were some fun times, even back then. I had a friend, Kay Hoffman, who had a car; we went on rides, that was a very big event for me.

"Hey, it's almost bedtime and Mick you've got to get out to the field for plowing tomorrow. See if you can make it up by 7:00, you lazybones!"

I gave Mom a kiss on the cheek, saying, "I can't wait," and a quick hug to Dad and headed to the bathroom to brush my teeth and pee, all this before tromping up to the steps to the bedroom where I would look at the latest "Sport" Magazine with Mickey Mantle on the cover and dream of being a big league player like him.

28

MOM (MOLLY'S) STORY – PART II

Mom's story was continued at another time. On another evening, yet that same summer, we were out on the porch again, this after one of my favorite times – making homemade ice cream out on the back stoop, my job to keep turning the handle on the wooden ice cream maker until it got hard to turn and we knew the ice cream was ready. The maker was a metal can with the "paddle" which I always got to lick, the can surrounded by ice from a bag from the ice plant and lots of rock salt thrown in. We always had thick cream, vanilla added to make that favorite flavor. Sometimes Mom would bring out a fresh bowl of strawberries from the garden to put on my heaping bowl of that good stuff. After putting her bowl to the side on the wooden porch floor, soon to be cleaned up by the pick tongue of one or two of the farm cats, she continued her story.

"After graduation from Sacred Heart, I returned to the farm at Kipp, not sure if I wanted to teach or not. In the fall I decided to go ahead and try it. In 1918 I rode out West on the train, accompanied by Mr. Donnelly as far as Colby. Then on to Kanorado near the Colorado line. Some people named Cody met me there and took me to a relative's house which was 18 miles from Kanorado into Colorado. The house was part sod, part wooden frame. We went to mass in Ray, Colorado, 25 miles to the northwest, an overnight trip. (I wondered, knowing Mom, did they ever miss mass?) At first, I earned 60 to 65 dollars per month, later on was to earn $125. Room and board were $20 per month.

"School was two miles from the farmhouse where I boarded. I walked or rode a horse to school. In winters we used a 'wagon-box sled,' a bobsled with runners, front and back. Crazy for the place and time, I recall a little boy student who brought me an orange each day to class. There was no water at the school; we had to go a quarter mile for water. My duties were to make the fire in the morning at the school in the coal stove. All this was before the teaching ever began.

"I remember that my students were good ones, although very poor. There was a poor family that lived on parched corn, a browned corn, like popcorn but not popped. I taught eight grades in the school. Boys were there part-time and worked on farms the rest of the time. (I remember Dad speaking of his schooling, a very similar situation. He studied through the eighth grade in the schoolhouse northeast of the farmhouse at Buckeye. He left school because he was needed on the farm.) The last day of school was always celebrated with a big dinner and a special program. This was between 1920 and 1923.

"Mick, enough for now. I'm tired. Next time I'll continue with the story and tell you about this handsome, Irish farmer and good Catholic who changed my life."

Next time came again on a summer evening on the front porch.

"In my third year after graduating from Sacred Heart I returned 'home' to teach in a country school eight miles north of Solomon, in Mom's (Minnie Callahan maiden name) area. I taught there for two and one-half years, suffering once from appendicitis. Then I returned to the same place as before in Colorado to teach, now in 1924. At this time I married Jones, and my son Paul (my half-brother) was born at Cameron, Missouri, east of St. Joseph. He was one and one-half when I left Jones, came home and that settled that. Jones was not a good man, was in fact a bad man who had deceived me badly, so I had to leave him.

"I later taught for one year, in 1929, in Woodbine, Kansas, southeast of Abilene. I did not like it, having to board in a filthy place with bad food; there were insects in the biscuit dough. And I was very lonesome at this time; Paul was living on the farm (where I grew up) at Abilene" (Note that the farm belonged then to Mr. Donnelly, Mom's mother's second husband. Donnelly had bought this farm in 1924 and had moved the family there from Kipp, Kansas. Mom said one of the main reasons for the move was the activities of the Ku Klux Klan which was very active around Kipp and was opposed to the Catholics. A man named Tobias sold the half-section, the farm one mile east of Abilene where I grew up to Mr. Donnelly in 1924 or 1925 for some $35,000. Donnelly had sold his place at Kipp for $16,000.

"At this time George Ryan, my brother, was in business college and worked for United Trust in Abilene. He later moved to Kansas City and then to Grand Island, Nebraska. During the time in Woodbine, I boarded during the week and would come home to the farm east of Abilene on weekends, riding as far as Chapman on Friday nights. My brother Leon would pick me up there and bring me to the farm at Abilene.

Then I moved once again. It was getting old. This time I taught school for three years at Sandburn School, a country school three miles east of Detroit and one mile north. I lived on the farm at Abilene during this time and drove a Studebaker back and forth, from 1930 to 1933.

Good for you to know some history of those horrible 1930s, Mick. One summer I, my Mom Minnie, and Paul went to Boulder, Colorado where I attended summer school. Teachers were expected to better themselves and summer school was the only way. We drove in the Studebaker and stayed overnight at Uncle Carl Fields' house in Kanorado, Kansas. The car broke down in a little town in western Kansas and delayed us, so later that day we got tired and pulled into a farm lane to sleep. Mick, there were no motels then in western Kansas. A thief came in the night and said, 'I want your gas.' He was a veteran on a veteran's march to Washington, D.C. during the depression days. Mick, those were terrible times for most people, no jobs for many, and on top of that what we now call the Dust Bowl. The veterans were trying to get to Washington to protest all the bad conditions.

"Then, finally, I taught at Kapp School, the school on Buckeye Road two miles north of Highway 40, (the building my Uncle Tim O'Brien, Dad's brother bought later on and moved up to his farm, this in 1934 and 1935).

"So I guess you've been waiting for this. I met your Dad at church in Abilene. We had known each other in recent years around Abilene. My step-dad Donnelly knew Dad because both of them had taken the 4th Degree in the Knights of Columbus together. We were married on May 28, 1935, at St. Andrews's by the then parish priest, now Monsignor Fahey. We went to Kansas City for our honeymoon, but there was rain and floods on the wedding day. We had planned a trip to the Ozarks, but it was too wet to go. We lived at first in an apartment in Abilene, then on to the house on Brady Street in northeast Abilene, and finally to the farm in 1942.

"That's my story. Your Dad will have to connect the dots from them until now, a big part of it when he owned and ran the cream station at the Union Pacific Depot in Abilene. I'm sure you won't remember anything at least until you were five or six, and that would have been in 1946 or 1947. I'm tired, too much talking of all this. Someone said, 'Just write it all down.'"

29

SEAN AND MOLLY MARRY – THE CREAM STATION

In May 1935, when Dad married Mom (a bit of that story is told by Mom later), he bought the cream station on the south side of Abilene. He did not want to live with his mother on the farm, so he bought the cream station from his brother Liam. Dad's brother Tim had moved back to the original farm at Buckeye at that time and lived with their mom, my grandma. I can barely remember her, so maybe my image of her comes just from the picture of her, a very heavy farm lady. Dad bought five acres of ground in northeast Abilene, just on the edge of the city limits. The earliest pictures of me, Mick, are from the yard of that house when I was a tiny baby, curly hair and being held by brother Paul. The cream station prospered.

In 1942, Mom's brother, Leon was discouraged with farming and wanted to move to Chapman or Herington, small, relatively near-by farm towns. The farm belonged to Minnie Ryan Donnelly, Mom's mom; Donnelly being her second marriage, the first was to Ryan. They had inherited it from Mr. Donnelly in 1930.

Dad kept the creamery until 1944 or 1945. There is an old photo showing me in bib overalls coming out of the screened door of the creamery, crying, and brother Joe is outside with a smirk on his face. I can't remember what Joe did, but I was mad! Dad said the creamery made him $300 a month clear in those days, a respectable income at the time. But federal programs were initiated and with the price of grain and feed up, the price of eggs and cream went down, so the farmers stopped raising so many chickens and dairy cattle. (I don't understand the logic of this today, but it was one of Dad's favorite themes: the government's sticking its nose into something working well and lousing it up. Another was the "millers." They were the root of all evil.)

30

HOBOES AND THE "HOBO JUNGLE"

Not all was peaches and cream on the farm. There were some fears and dangers.

I obeyed Mom and Dad most of the time. If I didn't it was sure to end up in trouble, and maybe a whipping from Dad's belt. This time I was in Junior High, so I was about twelve or thirteen, must have been 1953 or '54, the same time all of us guys from school were playing pee wee or little league summer baseball. Before I can talk about it, I've got to say what Mom and Dad had always taught us about strangers, and for that matter, dangers.

I don't know why, but it seemed like Mom did most of the talking about this. I'm sure Dad thought the same, but maybe just because she was around us more, and maybe because she had been a teacher so long and had to herd and scold kids, I dunno. There was always the saying at night before bed, "Go on upstairs, say your prayers, go to sleep and don't let the bedbugs bite." The idea of bed bugs or of a bogeyman never kept me from going to sleep. But there were three or four other deals that did. They will all come into this story eventually.

I never thought about it when I was twelve, but it must have been a natural mother's or dad's thing, an instinct to protect your kids. Thinking about it, I guess maybe there was a lot more about all this than I imagined. We lived on a farm near a small town, everybody pretty much knew each other, and the biggest crime was an occasional slit tire by some local punks, turning garbage cans over on Halloween (a big joke was the one about turning the outhouse over with someone in it, but I never did actually hear of such an incident) and traffic stuff like speeding 40 miles per hour on Buckeye with a 30 mile per hour limit, running a stop sign, or maybe high school kids painting the water tower. Crime was associated with bigger towns like nearby Salina or maybe the rough and tumble "entertainment" section of Junction City next to the Army Base at Fort Riley.

It boiled down to "strangers." Maybe "the crazy man" from the County Farm, its house high on a hill east of our farm. But mainly talk about hoboes. It was a once in a while thing as long as I can remember to see hoboes walking along the two-lane highway down the lane, U.S. Highway 40. They would be picking up beer bottles and pop bottles; both had a 2-cent deposit in those days. Heck, Joe, Caitlin and me were down there often enough, at the end of the farm lane, either waiting for the school bus in the morning or getting off and coming up the lane in the afternoon. We would see one of those guys once in a while. But you didn't say "hi" or "hey" to them and them not to you. I guess they weren't too proud to be picking up the bottles. The funny thing is we picked up some too and made enough for a pack of baseball cards and bubble gum in my case. But that wasn't too often.

I only remember once or twice when one of them would come up the lane to the farmhouse, come through the gate in the front yard and knock on the front door by the porch. Mom was always wary and had warned us to stay clear of them, but she never but ever refused them a paper plate of some kind of food, generally a couple of sandwiches, and maybe even a piece of pie, along with a glass of water in a paper cup. She might say later, maybe at the dinner table that evening, "There are a lot of folks worse off than we are, don't ever forget that. Put yourself in their shoes." Dad would chime in, "You know even in the midst of the worse times in the 1930s' Depression, we always had plenty to eat. I guess we were really lucky to be farmers; I think we ate a lot better than most folks. You just had to be sure you could make the mortgage payment on the land. Hard work and livestock and not being hit so bad this far north by the Dust Bowl helped out."

But there was another thing about hoboes, a whole lot scarier. Abilene, being a railway town with three major lines, two of them east-west clear across the country, was on the "main route" for train travelers, those who could afford the old Streamliners all the way down to the hoboes who rode the rails, mainly on the old box cars on the freight trains (Jimmy Rogers had a song, its title I think "Will There Be Any Box Cars In Heaven?"). I guess because of that Abilene had its own hobo camp, they called them "jungles," out on the southwest part of town, south of the UP tracks near the city limits. Everybody knew about it, but not too many people talked about it. The three-man police force and the county sheriff kept their eyes out for any trouble. That brings me to my story and some shenanigans.

Summer baseball was a democratic thing, although us guys would never have put it that way. "Rich kids," and I don' think anybody was rich, were from some families who were "well-off," had nice houses, new cars and maybe were members of the country club, the kids playing golf, and the rest of us, including a lot of farm kids, all played baseball. It didn't matter where you lived or what your Dad did. So we had three or four guys, all good friends, from the south side of the tracks. That just meant they went to Lincoln Grade School before we all ended up in the same Junior High. Heck, our local hero, General Dwight D. Eisenhower (we all had that name memorized) was a "south side" kid. One of my buddies, "Slim" Rivers (he was as skinny as I was), and another, Rip Warner, a big strong kid who would become our best football player, used to play regularly down on the Smokey Hill River south of town, catching huge "mudcat" cat fish in those brown, dirty waters, and not being afraid of snakes or snapping turtles or the like. Both Slim and Rip had grown up playing together and had at least visited the hobo camp.

We had all ridden our bicycles to baseball practice one of those summer mornings, had finished the infield, batting practice and pop fly practice, and Slim said, "Hey, let's go down to the hobo camp. It'll only take about fifteen minutes. Sometimes they'll give us match book covers from faraway places. And it's kind of like camping out." I had never camped out even once in my life; heck, farm life was like camping out every day. And I said, "Naw. I got to get home anyway. We're picking sweet corn this afternoon." Slim said, "I think you're just afraid. C'mon, it'll do you good to see how the hoboes live. Oh, if you've got a candy bar or snack with you, bring it along and we'll have something for them." So we all rode in a big bunch, Slim and Rip leading the way, but me and Luke as well, me bringing up the rear.

The camp was in a large grove of cottonwoods on the edge of town, no paved roads but a couple of graveled roads into it. We all got off our bikes and parked maybe a block away and Slim lead the way into the camp. There were several of those old army surplus heavy cotton duck tents, makeshift fire pits with rocks around them, and old shirts, pants and stuff hanging from ropes strung up in the trees to dry. They had a fire going in front of one of them, a spit across it and what looked like a can of beans hanging by a wire from the spit. Maybe five or six men were sitting around it. Most of them were smoking what looked like cigarette or cigar butts they must have picked up somewhere, they had on overalls and old muddy boots, and most needed a shave. Slim surprised the hell out of me, walking right up to the firepit, saying "Hey, I brought some friends along so they could see what your camp looked like. I've got a couple of candy bars, and they have some sandwiches and snacks too. Maybe you could dig up some of those cool match book covers or boxes you guys had last time I was here."

One of them, a mean looking guy if ever I've seen one, stood up and said, "Yeah I remember you from last time. Is it Slim?" "Yep," said my friend. "Let's see what you got." After putting the pretty modest bunch of candy bars, a couple of sandwiches and a banana into a sack, he said, "Hey you guys, check your pockets and see what we can give these guys.

We sure appreciate the grub, never enough to eat, nowhere, no time." Slim, ever the veteran, said, "Where do you all come from and where are you going?" "Not anywhere anytime soon. Our butts and backs are sore from those hard planks in the boxcars, just need a day or two to rest. I've rolled in from L.A., Shorty here came all the way from Seattle, and a couple of the guys are heading the other way, back from Chicago and St. Louis. We can do odd jobs if you've got any."

Just then, from out behind one of the tents, a grizzled, dirty guy in torn clothes, stepped out of the bushes where he must have been relieving himself, and smiled at us. He had one of those pint whiskey bottles in his hand and, holy shit, I saw what looked like a Bowie knife, in a sheath in his belt. He came toward us, swaying some, and said, "I bet these young fellows got some cash and some change on them too. How about it guys?"

Jack, the guy doing all the talking before to Slim edged toward the drunk guy and said, "Harry, these boys just came to see us, friendly like, even brought some snacks. Put away that bottle and go sleep it off." Harry took another swig, swaying even more and moved toward Jack, pulling the knife out of his belt. "Whoa Harry. Somebody's going to get hurt and it ain't going to be me." Suddenly the drunk veered the other direction toward Slim and took a wild swing at him, cutting the top of his arm in the process. That was when Jack jumped him and knocked him silly with a big old fry pan. I thought he was going to kill him, but the other guys dragged him off. Jack said, "We can't have no problems here with the fuzz; they'll run us all out. Don't worry about this creep on the ground. We'll hogtie him and hoist him aboard the next boxcar coming into the yard. He'll wake up in St. Louis and won't know what hit him."

Luke said, "Hey Slim I've got a couple of towels in my bike bag, let me get 'em and we'll wrap that arm." Fortunately, it was a minor cut across Slim's forearm, the drunk guy was in no shape to make a bigger swipe, but a cut just the same. Slim said, "I'll tell Mom I fell off the bike and cut myself, and it'll be okay. It's happened before. Luke, thanks for the towels, and guys, I'm sorry for getting us all into this mess. I thought it would be fun for you to see this place. Never had any problems before. Let's just get the heck out of here. Oh, a favor, mum's the word on all this. Better for all of us I think." No one disagreed with that; we all mumbled a "yeah," got on our bikes and pedaled home as fast as we could.

I never went back to a hobo jungle.

31

THE COUNTY FARM AND THE "CRAZY MAN"

I just told you about the hoboes and the "hobo jungle" where we had that scrape after summer baseball practice, and the guys who would walk up the farm lane and ask for a handout, but I didn't finish some other scary business on the farm.

On the section to the east of our half-section across the county road there was good, level, ground near the highway for planting. North of that there was a gradual hill and in the middle of it on top was what we called the "County Farm." Some people called it the "poor man's farm." It was an old three-story stone house off by itself. I never knew for sure what all was involved with the place but just knew one of our Abilene Aggies' 4-H projects was when we would generally go up there and sing Christmas Carols. I only remember doing it once or twice, so it's all a bit hazy. We would stand outside the main door, do our carols and someone would open the door and have hot cider or cocoa and some cookies for us. Then we would move on to old folks' homes in town.

So I never knew exactly who lived up there on the hill and why they were there. Mom and Dad said it was poor people who had no other place to go and no money to take care of them, and so it was a good thing. Me, the pragmatist, asked "How do they pay for it if the people have no money?" Dad said, "There's a county tax that we all pay; I think that handles most of it. But there is also state and even national money for such things." But talk among buddies just once in a while was that it was the place they put all the crazy people. I know there was a state mental hospital for problem kids out in western Kansas 'cause one of our schoolmates suddenly disappeared from Jr. High after he beat up somebody and pulled a knife on him, this downtown near the old "bad" pool hall.

I know what you're thinking. That Anthony Perkins movie "Psycho" had just come out, and all of us kids saw it at the Plaza movie theater in town. The shower scene with all the blood running down the wall and the creep that ran the motel gave me nightmares for two weeks.

It was sometime after that, maybe even a few weeks later, that it happened. It was in the middle of the summer, one of those hot Kansas nights, and we all had gone to bed early since there was field work to be done the next day. I of course was sleeping upstairs in that same old bedroom Joe and I had shared before he eventually went off to college. I don't know if Dad and Mom were sound sleepers or what but for whatever reason …

I'm a real sound sleeper, only time I have to get up is to pee, and I'll just pee out the east window through the screen rather than the ordeal of turning on all the upstairs, hall and downstairs lights to get to the old bathroom next to the kitchen on the first floor. Have you ever had a nightmare and woke up suddenly and not know exactly where you were or what was going on? It was like that. He was standing by the bed, not saying anything, just looking at me.

It didn't register at first because I was so groggy. Then I saw it was real. I screamed or yelled, "Dad, Mom help!!" The guy jumped, turned around and I heard him run down the hallway, take the stairs two at a time, and run out the front door, all this by the time Dad came running into the living room by the hall stairs with a rifle in his hand. I don't know what he was thinking, but he ran on outside, yelled, "Stop! I've got a gun on you. And it's loaded."

The man stopped and just stood there, not moving, not saying nothin' and maybe shaking a little like when you're shivering coming in from outside in the winter after doing all the barnyard chores. Dad, the gun still pointed at him, said, "Who are you? Where did you come from?" The guy just turned around a little and pointed East, the same direction as the County Farm. By this time Mom was in the doorway in her night robe and said, "Sean, I'm calling the sheriff."

In a few minutes the sheriff's car sped up the lane, pulled up, Sheriff Willerton got out, a pistol in his hand, and said, "Sean, sorry about all this. Old Ned has pulled this a time or two, wandered out of his room and the house and ended up down the county road, even down on old '40 once. He's never gotten into anybody's house before, so that's why we never talked to you. I'll talk to Mr. Hopkins the manager up there and I think it's time Ned was maybe moved down to Topeka for everybody's peace of mind. Is everybody all right?"

By this time, I was downstairs too, in my pijamas, looking out the front door. Mom put her arm around me and said, "Mick, it's all okay. The sheriff's here. We can all go back to bed. See if you can get some sleep. He wouldn't have hurt you."

Maybe, maybe not. I can tell you now that no one in rural Kansas, and not even in Abilene, locked their doors at night in those days. But the O'Briens started to lock up every night after that. And, oh, you probably already know, just a year later there was that horrible thing out in Western Kansas where those guys walked into a farmhouse and ended up killing everyone in cold blood.

The whole thing gave me the creeps and I sure as hell didn't sleep that night. We never heard of a psychiatrist or social worker in those days. You just dealt with stuff, but Dad and Mom, especially Mom would tell me, she saying her Rosary in the downstairs dining room by the heat register before going into bed, "Mick, the Good Lord is watching over us. The doors are locked, and besides, your Dad's got that gun beside the bed in the bedroom. In a few days all of this will wear off."

And it did, but I'm still telling you about it. I don't mean to make a big deal of it, but everything was just not milking cows and feeding the hogs in those days. It was about this same time, growing older, but still really young, that something else happened, a really big deal.

32

THE FLOOD OF '51

One of the most exciting times growing up on the farm once again was related to the elements. In 1951 we had the granddaddy of all floods in our area. Incessant rains caused all the small streams and the Smokey Hill River to rise; there were not that many rivers and streams around, but it doesn't take many. The biggest stream was the Smokey Hill River just south of Abilene, perhaps three or four miles from the south city limits. But there were small tributaries to it that could do more damage, like Mud Creek that flowed through the middle of town and Turkey Creek running through Brown's Park south of town.

The river and streams went well out of their banks that summer. From the high ground in the pasture in the upper part of our farm you could look south and see a huge band of muddy, brown water. It was of course a disaster for summer crops; the fields were flooded, but that is not the part I remember.

There were deer in Brown's Park south of town, and for some reason they ended up on the high ground of our farm. For the only time while growing up, we could go to the pasture and see those incredibly beautiful and graceful creatures in the wild. I can remember getting close to them and all of a sudden, they would kind of bounce on and easily vault the fence and head into the neighbor's pasture.

But it was better than that. The water also flooded the airport south of town, so the private planes had to be moved to higher ground. Our farm was chosen as a temporary landing and storage site, so we had maybe a half dozen single-engine planes parked on the slopes of the pasture. It was incredibly exciting for me to see them land and take off, I don't see how with the rough pasture, some terraces and lots of chuck holes. I guess they used the single lane road in the middle of the pasture we took up to get the cattle. The culmination was a ride in one over all the flooded area, the first time I had flown. It was a scary and exciting experience. I think it was then I began to dream of being a pilot. I know it was the same time as the Korean War, the evening Gabriel Heater newscasts and the "count" or "score" of the dogfights of Saber Jets and Russian Migs (and also the time in school when I would draw it all during penmanship class). I have loved flying ever since; had aptitude and eyesight worked out, I would surely have chosen that for a profession.

I can remember a strange, macabre dream I used to have as a boy and am sure it came from those days. It was about a crash landing of a commercial airliner in the pasture with me a hero helping people out of the plane that was a propeller type, maybe a DC-3 or the like.

But there was more fun from the flood. Brother Paul decided he would be a Good Samaritan, or else just tear ass around, so he put the scoop on the back of the little Ford tractor and off we went into the flooded town streets, ostensibly to give people rides across flooded streets and rescue damsels in distress. But from my vantage point, sitting propped up against one of the fenders, it was a neat way to plow through flooded streets, a barrel of fun.

We were also solicited for another reason during the flood. Town water was contaminated, and it was known we had very good well-water, so frequent cars from town would drive out to fill their jugs. It was just another bit of added movement and excitement in a small farm boy's existence. Mundane for most I'm sure, such memories are the stuff of Kansas in the 1950s.

There was little else for me to remember from the flood. Our summer ballgames were of course rained and flooded out, but mainly I remember it as a prelude to those next four or five years of serious drought and the hardships it brought to farmers all over the region, specifically to my Mom and Dad.

33

HARD TIMES, THE CARS

Part of telling of hard times with Mom and Dad was our cars. Caitlin and Joe were gone by then, Paul was working as an estimator at a small manufacturing plant in Enterprise that made passenger elevators for grain elevators. The cars tell a lot of the story.

When you are real young, you don't notice, but maybe by the time I reached Junior High in 1954 and 1955, I became aware of our economic situation, one of the ways was cars. We never did get around in the newest of cars; there was just no way Dad could afford them. My earliest recollection is a 1940s vintage Buick which was also the car in which we had the bad wreck in 1949. It was black, had four doors and a running board, a okay car, I guess, for the times.

The next car I recall was an old Plymouth, green if I'm not mistaken, or maybe yellow. This must have been a late 40s model as well. It's the one we were hauling the trailer with when Wilhelmina my Sears Gilt 4-H hog hit the road. I was aware we had these old vehicles and as I write this now I regret my immaturity because I recall bugging Dad to do this and that about the cars, to get some things fixed, and I am sure the maintenance he did or did not do depended much on the little money he had available. But we never had the shiny new cars around.

Oh, maybe not related but the cars make me think of it. Another thing was clothes. I think I would complain about not having enough nice clothes. Boys wore blue jeans and t-shirts to school, even up through high school in the late 1950s, although I remember dressing more then, partly because I had become very aware of girls. But our jeans were from J.C. Penney and not from Keels which had Levis. Just an accidental memory, one time playing with a friend in town we were in the house and his bedroom to see his baseball card collection, and there was an open closet – he had stacks of underwear shorts and t-shirts, all clean and ready to go in the closet. That made an impression on me.

The first memory I had of dressing up was Mom buying me a purple corduroy sport coat, grey slacks, pink shirt and dark tie for what I think was my first junior-high dance. My buddy Luke Zimmerman who lived on the farm across the road had the same outfit, so I guess the farm wives got together. I think the colors were "in" then; it might have been influence from Elvis Presley.

The only other "dress up" clothes were what I thought was an elegant dark striped suit I wore while on the high school debate team that won the state championship in 1959, just recently. So I had some good clothes. I can recall that Caitlin made many of hers; Mom was a good seamstress and with a sewing machine, 4-H and all, girls were expected to learn to sew.

Back to the cars. I never had a car in high school, but a few of my friends did. Thinking back on it, it was the kid from Enterprise whose family owned the elevator company my brother Paul worked for so many years who had the shiny new 56 Chevy (he had it up to over 100 miles per hour driving us to a basketball game in McPherson), or the farm kid from north of town who had the 57 Ford Fair Lane white convertible. But it was mainly the "less popular" kids who did not do sports or debate or school stuff that had cars, oftentimes "hot rods," and spent their time customizing them with pin stripes, duel tail pipes for lots of noise and working to pay off the cars. They tended to be the same ones into drinking and smoking earlier on. I did have the use of the family car for dating during junior and senior years in high school. I cannot recall for sure what kind of car we had then but cannot remember feeling ashamed of it. I always washed and polished it before a date.

Paul was the one who always had a nice car, but he worked full time as long as I could remember. When he was in one of his prosperous periods (and there were real ups and downs in his life in those days), he bought Dad and Mom a '58 green Chevy, stick shift, pretty plain. That was the first time we had ever had a new shiny car.

I wasn't always an angel. It was about this time when brother Joe was working construction during summer off school in Lehigh, a little town south of Abilene, near Hillsboro. I drove down to pick him up in that new 58 Chevy. I decided it was a good time to see what the car would do, and I know I had it up to 100 to 105 on a two-lane hilly highway. I was a good driver, careful and not reckless, but when I think of that now I shudder. Joe just said, "How did you get down here so fast?"

Paul once had a tiny, red MG roadster, not the "classic," but the one with rounded fenders, a real beauty. He lent it to me one afternoon and I promptly drove by the local swimming pool where the blooming high school girls hung out and put a dent in the fender watching them instead of where I was going while backing out of the parking spot beside the pool. I was scared shitless when I drove up the farm lane and parked the MG in the barnyard in front of the house. Paul was inside and I walked up to him, gave him the keys and said, "I'm really sorry but I had a bit of an accident." Amazingly enough Paul, said, "Oh? Let's go outside and look." We walked out, he saw the dent in the shiny red fender, looked at me, and laughed! He said, "Mick, I'm not sure there will be a next time. Good thing I've got insurance. Don't believe you are quite ready for driving my car." He did not yell, scream or lay hands on me, and I wonder how I would have reacted if in his place. Lots of memories have smells; I remember the leather smell of that car's interior.

Time passed.

34

DROUGHT, 'HOPPERS, RAIN AND HAIL, SEAN IN FLORIDA

It must have been about that time, since I know you got your driver's license at age 14 in Kansas, and now about 1955, there was a lot more going on just keeping the farm going, and I, Mick, was becoming more aware of Dad's situation on the farm. I think he made a little money in the good years, suffered in the bad years, but managed to keep things afloat. I need to recall that he and Mom grew up during the Depression, so hard times were nothing new.

It always sticks in my mind that good dry land wheat made about 25 to 30 bushels to the acre in those my growing up days in the 1940s and 1950s, perhaps at $1.00 per bushel. There was that terrible flood in 1951 that was followed by four or five disastrous years of drought. Those I recall well because I was older and more aware of things.

I can recall the grasshopper years when they came in clouds and destroyed everything, particularly the alfalfa and corn crops. I recall the rig Dad as well used to spray with: a 50-gallon barrel with hoses, etc. on the back hitch of the little Ford tractor, riding along in the field, so tiny he seemed, spraying the fields. It never seemed to do much good. I can still see in mind's eye today the alfalfa sprigs with no leaves on them, with as many as four or five 'hoppers on each stem. The hoppers came and went, but it was drought that seemed to bring them most.

During the series of bad years, early and mid-1950s, Joe and Caitilin were in high school, I was in Junior High, there were wheat crops that came to only 5 to 7 bushels to the acre, and wheat was the primary source of revenue, the cash crop on the farm. And it was not only the drought. One of the most vivid memories of all my childhood also happened just around wheat harvest time in one of those years.

One summer, it must have been late June or even early July, very close to harvest time, the wheat was headed out and Dad expected in fact a bumper crop (this could not have been the dry years but must have been wet years which immediately followed). We had lots of rain which eventually would knock down the wheat and could cause no end of problems - a rust or growth on the wheat, kernels knocked from the head, etc. The fragility of farming strikes me once again, the fine line between too much rain and not enough, too much sunshine or not enough. The ideal was good rain to start the wheat in the fall, snow cover in the winter for gradual moisture and to protect from blowing winds, steady spring rains in March and April, then lots of sunshine for ripening. This particular day we all saw the cloud coming, Dad, Mom and I. It was grey, almost whitish, and came from the southwest. The cloud advanced slowly, wind and rain preceding it. I was alone with Mom and Dad that day (Joe and Caitlin by then were working in other towns or in Abilene), and we saw the hail literally mow down the prospective bumper crop. For my Dad, there were no tears, no yelling, no raving or jumping up and down, but just a sad resignation. I just remember him saying, "Let's go back to the house and get out of the hail and rain." (I wonder with my own personality how I would have dealt with that.) My worst fears this time were not to come to be. Dad had crop insurance, hail insurance. Ordinarily this kind of insurance would never insure a profit, but you could at least recoup some of the expenses in planting, tilling the soil, etc. But this time there was a bonus - the hail did not knock the wheat from the head or knock the head off; instead it broke and bent the stalks, bending the head low to the ground. Dad was able to use what we called a "pickup" attached to the front of a combine and recover much of the wheat that went ahead and ripened. But the sight of the force of nature, that white cloud, the heavy hail that clipped the wheat like swinging a baseball bat through a patch of weeds, breaking them off but not cutting them off, remains in my memory.

Worse of course were the droughts when the wheat was thin in the fields, when there was only one crop of alfalfa instead of three or even four cuttings, and when the corn dried up in the fields and the only thing to be done was to cut it for silage, at least partially salvaging the crop. In the middle of all those years there was one particular period of crisis, a time of severe drought. It was in 1955 when I was in the 8th grade of Junior High. To keep things going Dad did part-time and even full-time carpentry in town, this plus keeping the farm going. He later would lease the farm ground, taking shares, and actually come out better dollar wise than when he had farmed it himself. I think one of his brothers farmed it a year or two, the next-door neighbor the rest; I was happy for Dad in those last years because the backbreaking and frustrating work was over. He told me once that even then he would have continued to farm if he had had the money to get up to date machinery; he simply did not. But I'm getting ahead of myself.

Back to 1955; the carpentry jobs became scarce and then suddenly ended. I think Dad was helping Caitlin in college at the time; things were rough. The only solution was to follow one of the local contractors (Dad had worked for him building houses out west of Abilene) to Melbourne, Florida, along the Atlantic coast, where the contractor had work. Dad made the "migration" just to keep working and to keep some money coming in.

So that winter Dad left Mom and me on the farm and worked in Florida (Caitlin and Joe were away at school.) I did not, once again, truly realize the gravity of the situation. But I know Mom would get the weekly letters with the check inside and would just say "I wish Dad were here." Indelibly printed on my memory was the morning I came downstairs and saw Dad in the kitchen, looking so much older, tired, oh so tired. He must have been about 63 or 64 at the time. He had been on the bus for two days, arriving from Florida. I did not know initially why he was home, if the job there had ended, if there still was a need for it, but I was so glad to see him. This, as far as I know, was the only time he and Mom were separated in their marriage. I cannot recall if there was a big hug or even an emotional moment, but only the relief that Dad was home. But that was when I began to realize that he and Mom were not so young anymore.

I think Mom and Dad were good managers of the little they had to work with. I know they had to be frugal and wise or they would not have made it. They had limited experience about money matters (in an urban, educated sense of investments), because they had little money or opportunity to use it. But I know Dad studied a lot about farming methods, farm management and kept an open ear to new techniques. He kept a close eye on farm market conditions and prices. He would attend the county extension meetings for stuff like that and always had a couple of farm magazines on subscription. And he never missed the farm and Farm Bureau news on the radio.

35

WINTERTIME AND SNOW, HUNTING AND GAMES

Snow and the Wintertime. Serious stuff, but fun and games and hunting. We normally did not get a heavy winter in Abilene; by that, I mean the kind of winter where it snows in November and there is snow on the ground until late April. But you knew when winter had arrived in the area, the first light snow perhaps in December, and always with the hope for a white Christmas. Sometimes a heavy snow would come along. There had been hard freezes since early November. January, February and very early March were plenty cold and potentially nasty with possibilities of heavy snow. We have what they had always called blizzards - that meant a heavy snowstorm with strong winds which caused the snow to drift. When that would happen, it could be serious: livestock had to be protected.

And sometimes we could not get the one mile into town for a day or two. Pipes would freeze up, the water tank for the animals too, and a bitter cold would envelop things for a few days. I can remember the ax we would keep down at the stock tank to break up ice so the stock could drink.

The snow cover was always good for the wheat which had been planted in September; it provided slow and easy moisture when it gradually melted in the Spring and protected from blowing dust in dry weather.

There are many memories associated with our winter - freezing hands trying to milk the cow and do other chores in the morning; using the ax to chop the ice on the livestock water tank; frozen clothes on the clothesline, including cold, wet jeans on your body when you were heading off to school; there was no such thing as an electric clothes dryer on the farm. Water pipes even in the house would freeze up; lots of inconvenience to say the least. I wonder how Dad and Mom handled it all. I remember particularly getting into freezing cars to go into town. You almost always went out, started the engine and heater just to make it livable. But I can recall often sitting in a freezing car and seeing your breath until the car warmed up.

I can recall two or three bad blizzards, one in 1950 or 1951 when the Fields were visiting from Goodland, Kansas in their big, shiny Buick. There was one winter when all of us kids got Scarlet Fever; Mom and Dad moved one of the big beds down to the first floor living room. For me it was actually a happy time; no one could go out or leave, so we were forced to play together. I remember long, long Monopoly games, card games. The memories are fuzzy now, but I think Caitlin, Joe and I were all sick.

I can remember driving on snow and ice to get to school. When the winds and heavy snow combined, inevitably there would be serious traffic problems on old Highway 40, at that time the major east-west road through Kansas. I can recall one time when the highway was a sheet of ice about 4 to 5 inches thick with snow on the top. We would put on boots, gloves, coats, etc. and go down to the highway to see it all. I guess the people in those vehicles were all right; you heard of people freezing to death in cars and trucks along highways in western Kansas and eastern Colorado, and the panhandle in Oklahoma and western Nebraska.

Midwest ice storms happened less frequently yet, but a freezing rain would leave tree branches, telephone and electric lines coated with ice, and the weight would cause them to break and create problems in the area. But the morning after an ice storm was a beautiful thing to see: the first rays of the morning sun coming through the clouds and the shimmering branches, and even the ice on the grass.

Back to the big snowstorms. After a particularly heavy snow, a day or two later, it was great fun for the kids when we would bundle up in galoshes or boots, and maybe an extra pair of pants (blue jeans or better yet, corduroy pants), sweaters, coat, gloves and winter hat to play in the big drifts along the road. Later on, when the deep snow would begin to melt, it also was fun to have the rushing water in the culverts and play games jumping across them, or sailing pieces of wood down them. Of course if the storm was bad enough, they would call off school. We always hoped for that and listened to the radio the preceding night or early the following morning for the road and school closures. That meant a day at home playing in the snow or inside with games. Monopoly was my favorite growing up, and I have good memories of all the kids including Paul in on those games. We never considered the fact that all those days had to be made up later, generally in gorgeous spring weather when we rather would have been outside playing ball.

When we were very young, we would build snowmen in the yard, using a carrot for its nose, and maybe a piece or two of coal for the eyes. But there was one winter we had extra fun; I cannot recall at exactly what age. There was an old sled with runners on it which was stored up above the beams in the granary. Paul pulled it down and hitched it to the little Ford tractor. We drove crazily through the pasture, upsetting us and landing in fairly deep snow, but never noticing the wet or the cold, just having a good time. I can only remember one time we did that, but what fun! Paul had a mischievous streak in him, and I think the sharp turns and upsetting us was all part of the plot.

I can remember hunting some in the winter, primarily rabbits. It seemed a lot more fun when you could see the fresh tracks in the snow and follow them to their lairs. I cannot remember hitting many of them, but we did have fried rabbit once in a while, most of them shot by either Joe or Dad.

My job was to hold the legs of the rabbit while Joe would skin it, a bit more than I wanted to handle at the time.

Maybe a little off the subject, but this makes me think of hunting and games the rest of the year. What I recall more easily and with great relish were my play days on the farm. I was allowed at a certain age, perhaps ten or eleven, to take the Springfield Rifle single shot or even the 22 Special (shorts, long rifle) pump action out for "hunting." I was careful and had learned good habits with the rifles, but it still was a game to me. Since I never seemed to hit much during hunting, I would rather just shoot ricochet shots to hear the same sound I used to hear in the Roy Rogers movies. You know, the "pteeeerr" sound of the glancing bullet. My favorite game for quite a while was cowboys and Indians, me being the only player and with the only rifle. The villains were Indians – maybe Iroquois or Hurons, the ones I had seen in movies like "The Iroquois Trail" who shaved their heads except for a single swath down the middle. I've said I used to draw marvelous pictures of them in school when I should have been paying attention to the teacher, entire battle scenes with Iroquois and buckskin fringed heroes a la Daniel Boone or Davy Crockett. As I write this, I just remembered the haircuts in style when I was a kid, the "Mohawks" which meant a shaved head with a swath down the middle; I never had one, can't say if for lack of courage or fear of a spanking at home.

Anyway, I had a set route I would take: through the hole in the fence between the chicken house and the tree stump where we cut off the chicken heads, through the windbreak of cedar trees Dad had painstakingly planted over the years, past the "coffee bean" trees, through the buffalo grass meadows in the long pasture which gradually ascended to a hill from which you could see the entire valley. I always stopped to rest at that point, gazing out over the cropland down toward the highway and the Smokey Hill River beyond. There were little gullies or ravines that inevitably had Indians in them or varmints of one sort or another. I could use half a dozen shells by that time. But the highlight of the game took place near the pond on the north 40 acres. A great place to play, it was surrounded by large elm trees and many other kinds Dad would gradually plant over the years. Generally, there was just a little water in the pond since it had always seeped some. Dad spent lots of hard-earned money trying to fix that, even going so far as to buy some sealer to put on the bottom of the pond. But there were lots of birds, an occasional duck or crane or heron, squirrels and the like. My game of Daniel Boone and the Iroquois might be interrupted off and on, perhaps finding an old tin can to use for target practice. But many, many times I would take off alone from the house with the explanation that "I was going hunting," but would play that game instead. (I wonder how my folks must have worried with an eleven-year-old out with the rifle alone.) But there were no people around and big distances on the farm.

The other game, at an earlier age, involved wild animals in an African jungle (a carryover from the black and white Tarzan movies with Johnny Weissmuller or the Jungle Jim comics). There was a small field of about 5 acres south of the farmhouse that Dad usually planted in brome grass and let livestock use for pasture. The brome grass grew tall, and even taller was the sunflowers and miscellaneous weeds. I would roam that field playing games of Tarzan and the jungle and did some climbing on a large outdoor sign near the highway, a sign rented by the local Chevy - Cadillac dealership. I must have been ten years old or less for those games. There were all sorts of wild animals and critters lurking behind trees, fence posts, and in the tall grass. At some point I would carry a machete, a real one, another item Paul brought home from the Army Air Force Service and cut my way through the jungle debris.

However, the field became less pleasant for me in later teenage days when Mom or Dad would send me along the fence with a hoe or machete to cut down those same weeds, particularly sunflowers or cockleburs which seemed to proliferate along the roads in Kansas.

36

BUDDIES, FUN AND GAMES

Life was not all hard times and sad times, far from it. I think from the time maybe when I was ten years old in 1951 on up through the 1950s no boy in America, and for sure no farm boy, ever had so much fun. A lot of it was due to living near such a small town and maybe that was the reason it was easy to make friends, but also an awful lot due to me, Mick, having a really good imagination. There's a lot I want to tell here about all that.

As I grew up there was a continual string of buddies I would invite to play on the farm. My nearest brother Joe was four years older than myself, and by the time I was old enough to play sports, he was already much larger and had other interests. Although I can remember games of basketball and some football with Joe, and of course that boxing lesson, I had the definite idea most of the time that my older brother and sister really did not want to spend much time with me. So it was simple - either play alone or have friends my age over from town. The games we played were centered on sports and those in season. Baseball was the vacation time sport in the summer and at my place basketball predominated through Fall, Winter and Spring.

Bob Gerson came to be a good friend. He was not one of the more popular kids in school, was a bit slow in his studies, but his athletic abilities were more on a par with mine, average or a little above, speaking for Abilene. We would spend hours playing ball in the summertime on the farm, primarily catch, each pretending to be a major league pitcher. I never did learn to throw a curve ball, much as I wanted to, and neither did he, but we pretended to!

Bob's dad Jeff was a good man who coached the little kids in summer baseball for years. He had done some semi-pro playing in the area and it was always rumored that he had been big league material until he threw out his arm as a catcher. He coached a couple of the little league teams I played on as a kid. The teams were Ehrsams and Dairy Queen. One memory from the former, we must have been 10 or 11 years old, tells it all.

I had a pretty good arm for being such a skinny rail of a kid, so I became our catcher; I could actually throw runners out at second or third if they dared to try it. Maybe because of that, in one of the games, and we had a lousy team and were real far behind, we ran out of pitchers. Jeff came up to me between innings and said, "Mick, Bob is going to catch next inning; I'm going to give you a try at pitching. Just throw the ball over the middle of the plate." Long story short, I said, "Geeze Coach Jeff, I'll give it a try." I warmed up like I knew what I was doing but proceeded to not even get one out. Walked four guys in a row and don't know yet if I ever threw a strike. End of game, end of maybe a dream I'll tell about later, but I recall just laughing after Jeff took me out: "Hey I just threw a no hitter. And no home runs either."

Another time was maybe a year later, and it was night and day. We were all a year older, Jeff was still the coach, but we that summer we had what we used to call a "PHENOM," a fire balling country pitcher. By this time, still with a good arm, I was playing third base, he threw to me, a pick off move or something, and the force of the throw literally knocked me on my butt on the bag. He had to be the pitcher that year with Dairy Queen, I think, because we were undefeated. The fun of it all was that after the game all of us were treated to whatever we wanted at the local DQ - a big strawberry malt or hot chocolate sundae or the likes, a great reward for sitting on third base.

A couple of years later, now maybe in junior high or high school, I played catcher again and we had another fire-baller. My main memory is my left hand would be all swollen up after a game of his pitches; I used to put small sponges in the mitt to help out with that. He went on to college pitching.

37

JEREMIAH WATSON

Another really good buddy was Jeremiah Watson; he was connected to the whole story of music in our family and my efforts to learn to play the guitar when we both were fourteen and freshmen in high school at ole' AHS, Abilene Public High School. Jeremiah and I wangled our way out of afternoon study hall (don't ask me how) and went to the band room maybe three or four times a week, tuned up our guitars and played white music - the Everly Brothers (Jeremiah could harmonize for second voice, I never could get the hang of it), Elvis Presley's big hits, tunes from the top 40 radio programs, including Ricky Nelson. I don't know how good we got or how good we could play, but the high point of all that was when sister Caitlin wangled a way for us to play up at Marymount College in nearby Salina, a school run by the old time Sacred Heart Nuns with the black long habits, white collar just above the eyebrows and a big string of rosary beads at their waist. Caitlin had transferred there when I was a sophomore in high school. The nuns had a good reputation as teachers. Anyway, Caitlin arranged for me and Jeremiah to come up and play in the cafeteria after dinner. I remember the scene: we have on cowboy hats, jeans, but no cowboy boots; I'm sure we didn't own any. Jeremiah is a hoot; he looks a lot more natural in one of those old bluesmen beat up fedoras than a too small straw cowboy hat. It must not be too bad 'cause they let us sing about every song we know and even an encore. It wasn't a real long program.

But there's a lot more to it than music. I can honestly say that although I was aware of differences between Negro and White then, that there was little or no prejudice in me. Jeremiah was a good friend with qualities other friends did not have. I recall having him out to the farm to play music, but also for the same sports as with other buddies. Perhaps it was a coincidence, but he was also "just average" in sports. Neither of us could throw a curve ball, but we could play a decent game of catch. My parents did not object to having a black friend out to the farm, but it turned out to be an uncommon thing to do in our town in those days, although I certainly did not realize it at the time. I guess it was a surprise to me sometime that year in high school when the class bully came up to me in the hall and said, "Mick you shithead Irish punk, you think you're so goddamned smart and too good for us real country guys, why are you having that nigger out to your place to play ball, and hell, you've never asked me?" I blurted out, "Because he's a 'helluva lot smarter, nicer, and talented than you, you red-neck son of a bitch." Butch looked at me kind of funny like and hauled off and punched me in the mouth. Tasting blood, I guess I got mad, all 114 pounds of me, and tried to swing back and might have nicked him on the chin. Just then Rip the big football player who had seen it all, ran over, said, "Butch, try picking on someone your own size for a change. C'mon let's go outside." Butch said, "As far as I know you ain't a nigger lover like Mick this Irish cat licker here, so I got no problems with you.," He backed off and went out the door by the cafeteria, yelling as he ran out the door, "Mick, this ain't the end of this." He walked over to his hot rod and peeled out of the parking lot. I went into the rest room and swabbed my face with a wet paper towel; there was some blood, a cut lip, but no broken teeth. Luke, and some other friends all came up to me, saying "Damn, Mick, we didn't know you had it in you. Next time give a yell and call us over. We would have made quick work of that duck-tailed hood."

Jeremiah came up, he had been down at the band room practicing his regular "gig" - trumpet with the high school band. Rip didn't give me a chance to talk but blurted out. "Jere, you owe Mick one; he took it on the chin for you, tackling ole' Butch in the hallway by the gym." Jeremiah seemed a bit slow to recognize the situation (you had to be careful anytime when you were five out of 400 in a white man's school), but said, "Mick, I won't be forgetting this. You prove there are some nice people in Abilene. Thanks, good buddy."

38

THE EBENEZER FIRST GOSPEL CHURCH

It might have been that, maybe making us closer friends, but it led to something really fun and then crazy a few weeks later. I don't think I've said, but Jeremiah lived in a tiny house in the small black part of town, just north of the old high school football field. There were probably only a couple of dozen black folks in town — we all knew the Wyatts as a very respectable family with good athletes and good students and music scholarships to college. Other black guys were the garbage collectors and yet another man who became prosperous with his own two or three semis that he hauled cattle in. We had ridden by the Watson house many times on bicycles from school or baseball practice, and Mom had given Jeremiah a ride home a time or two from playing on the farm. On one of those occasions his Mom Stella came out on the front porch, came out to the car, and said, "Jeremiah, your Pop's got chores for you, so I'll see you inside." After he had run up the steps and into the house, she said, "Mrs. O'Brien and Mick, I don't know how to tell you this, but I know Jeremiah never would. He comes home so happy and excited after a visit to the farm. And I guess you need to know this is the first and only time he's ever been on a farm. We black folks don't know too many farmers. I just want to thank you Mrs. O' Brien for raising your boy to be so kind. I know you are Catholics, and we've always been suspicious of them, but more than that you are good people. Thank you from the bottom of my heart." Mom said, "Jeremiah is a good boy and he and Mick have lots of fun. I hope they can continue to be good friends." I just said, "Mrs. Watson, me too."

It was probably a few weeks after that that I got my nerve up one day and was talking to Jeremiah and said, "Hey Jere, you know I know your Dad's a preacher and you don't ever say much about it, but I've seen that little church by your house. I've never been to a black person's church, but I'd sure like to go. Can you talk to your Dad about it?"

Jeremiah said, "Mick, no white person has ever been in church with us. I don't know if you know how touchy a thing like that can be in this town. Pa makes his living as a janitor at all those stores downtown; if he didn't have that, we'd probably starve and at least would have to move. He says 'yes sir' to everybody, has keys to some of the best stores in town, and brings home enough to pay the rent and groceries. But he's happy when it's Saturday night and he's in front of our friends preaching the good news and leading a hymn or two. I've never been to your church either, but I suspect it's a lot different from ours. If you still want to come, I'll talk to him, but you got to know it's pretty different from anything white folks do. I guess you'd say, it's poor and we're poor."

"Jere, maybe you don't know, but some people in town think we're rich just because we have a half section of land. What they don't know is that we have a big garden tractor to do all the work instead of a 'normal' Farm All or John Deere, old equipment that breaks down all the time, don't even have a pickup truck, and there are many years when we just barely make the mortgage payment, especially with the drought and all just these last years. Believe me, I'm not too rich to go to church with you. Hell, I wear Penney's jeans and a t-shirt and tennis shoes to school, and I guess just like you, have never been to the country club (and don't' want to), so let's just see if this works out."

Jeremiah said, "Okay Mick, I'll let you know. But you'll have to put on church clothes, dress shoes, pants and a white shirt if you come. I'll talk to Pa."

A couple of weeks later at school Jere said, "Mick, it's all set. Do you want to come this Saturday night? If your folks can drop you off, we'll find someone to take you home."

And so it was. I put on my black dress shoes, white shirt, blue dress slacks, combed my hair and Dad dropped me off in front of Jere's house. He was out on the porch to meet me. We walked right over to the three wooden step entrance to the church or hall, and Jere's Mom and Dad greeted us at the front door. Mr. Watson said, "Mick, this is a pleasure for us and maybe a thank you for all you've done for Jeremiah. I'm thinking you might be more comfortable toward the back of the hall, and Jere here will sit with you until the hymns begin. You will know a few friends from school, and everyone knows you are coming. I know you are a religious person and a good person, so it's no different here. Just listen to the word of the Lord."

The hall or church was like Jere said, very poor looking when you compare it to a Catholic Church, even a small one like St. Andrew's in Abilene. The walls were covered with a plain, dark colored wallpaper, and there were just three windows on each side covered with curtains. The front (there was no altar) was a low stage one step up, all wooden floor with a wooden pulpit to one side, leaving enough room for other parts of the service to the side. And there weren't any statues or crosses or anything like that. Lighting was four bare bulbs with shades hanging from the ceiling. There were home-made wooden pews on either side of an aisle, all plain too. Other than a straight back chair and small table at the entrance with a tiny square "vestibule," that was the Ebenezer First Gospel Church.

The hall, really one fairly large rectangular room, was pretty well filled when we went in and sure enough, I recognized most people, maybe not knowing their names, but in our small town you saw nearly everyone at some time or other on the street or at the sport contests like football and basketball. Three or four classmates from the high school saw me and smiled but did not wave. It was pretty quiet and a hushed atmosphere.

Then with a rustling sound about ten persons in dark blue robes walked up the center aisle and took places in the front pew. Mr. Watson (I should say Reverend Watson) then walked up the aisle, dressed in a long flowing black robe, walked to the pulpit, and the service started. Jere was right, it was night and day from a Catholic Mass. Mr. Watson started with a simple statement, "We have a special guest tonight, one of Jeremiah's school mates and best friends, please welcome Mr. Michael O' Brien." Much to my surprise, everyone stood, applauded and I even heard a "Thank you Jesus" and "Thank you Lord." Everyone sat down and Reverend Watson continued with a long prayer, all standing, "Let us pray." Then he opened a Bible and begin what seemed to be a never-ending reading of Scripture, first from the Old Testament and then the New.

Up to now I'm just starting to be a bit tired, but then it all changed. The Reverend welcomed the "choir," those ten robed people in the front row, and the place was transformed into a swaying, happy place. With no accompaniment (unlike that big organ in the loft in Catholic St. Andrew's) other than two tambourines, they sang what I think was about four hymns, warming up from a slow piece to a loud, fast piece with all singing and clapping in unison. The folks in the pews clapped and sang as well. The first hymn, "Nobody Knows the Trouble I've Seem" seemed mournful and recalled to me what I imagined were black folks' slave days.

To my surprise, then they stopped, and the Reverend took off with what amounted to a fire and brimstone sermon. I can't remember what the theme was, but I remember names – "Jesus," "Gabriel Blow Your Horn," "Michael the Archangel Defend Us," Out! Beezebub!" "The Fires of Hell," "Repent of Your Sins" and "Lord, Lord, Have Mercy on Us." It must have gone on for thirty minutes.

We weren't done yet. Reverend Watson, sweating profusely from the sermon, stopped, pulled out a white hankerchief, and announced, "All of you who have been saved please come up for a blessing and a laying on of hands. The Spirit is with us tonight. And anyone who wants to be saved, feel free to join us." So everyone, adults and children, filed up to the front center and bowed down in front of Reverend Watson, received his blessing and filed back to their seats. All this time the choir was singing quiet songs of praise. No one in line seemed new and not saved.

All of a sudden, it came to my row; all the people on my left stood up and began to go down the aisle. Jeremiah next to me said, "Go ahead. It's expected. Pa won't hurt you!" And he snickered under his breath. I'm thinking okay, I'm Catholic; we aren't supposed to even be in another church without permission, maybe a wedding or a funeral, and much less take part. It's a sin. Think fast. I'm a guest. Go ahead and get the blessing, might be as good as Father Fahey's. I followed the leader to the front and when Reverend Watson saw me, he said under his breath, "Good boy. I'm thinking you should kneel down, and I'll just put my hand on your head for a moment."

I have no idea what happened. Being that "good boy," I did as he said, knelt down and the next thing I knew two of the choir, tall men in robes, had ahold of me on either side under my shoulder, lifted me to my feet, and the whole time singing out loud, "Thank you Lord. Thank you, Jesus. Thank you, Jesus." They slowly walked me back to my seat and I just sat quiet for a while, feeling kind of dizzy, but at the same time, darn, like all my burdens had been lifted from me, kind of free. Suddenly there was polite applause, many shouts of "Praise Jesus, thank you Jesus," and all were smiling at me. Reverend Watson walked up to the pulpit and shouted, "Lord be praised. Mick, thank you for trusting in me and the Lord. Friends, this young whippersnapper has just been 'slain in the spirit.'" "Amen, amen, amen" and the choir launched into a joyous, foot stomping, clapping rendition of "Swing Low Sweet Chariot."

Soon the service concluded, we all filed out, and Reverend Watson said, "Michael, we don't have a new or fancy car, but my old Studebaker will get you home. Okay? How are you feeling? I hope there are no regrets from joining us."

"Reverend Watson, no, none, it's been an eye opener; never had this experience or felt like this. Don't tell Father Fahey I was here. I'm thinking he either would want to do an exorcism on me or more likely be a little jealous of you. I'm ready to go home. Thank you."

"Michael, what happens here stays here, don't worry. I believe you were indeed blessed by the Holy Spirit this very evening. I am happy to have been a witness and I'll never forget it. God bless you. Hold on just a minute and we'll drive you home. Jeremiah will come along; you two can give me directions although I know the farm is out east of town on Highway 40. You can tell me where to turn in." Lady the Border Collie barked in the yard at the strange car and Dad turned on the porch light. When I got out, he waved, walked back in, and I muttered a quick thank you to Reverend Watson and a bye to Jeremiah and soon did the same.

39

MUSIC AND THE FAMILY

All the business with Jeremiah made me think of more music, but at home with the family.

We were a musical family, largely through the inspiration of Mom who played the piano growing up. The upright piano we had in the "music room" in the southeast corner of downstairs was not serviceable most of the time as far as I can remember, being at least partially out of tune, with some keys unplayable. But Mom still wanted us to do music, and there was a long sequence of events and instruments.

Paul, as far as I know, never did an instrument, but had the best voice of all of us, but Caitlin, Joe and I were not bad at all. Paul sang in the school choir, operetta and in the Catholic Church choir when the singing at mass was Gregorian chant. I can still remember the different parts of the high mass, particularly where the bass-baritone voice of my brother came in. Paul sang at weddings, generally doing the Ave Maria. But his real specialty was "I'll take you home again Kathleen" at the reception, generally after getting well juiced up and lubricating the vocal cords.

Joe did the trumpet (he had a good voice as well, more tenor than Paul's, in school chorus and some school plays as well) and was in different local school bands, and I think still played as a NROTC cadet at Marquette in the drum and bugle corps in the late 1950s. Joe had gotten a naval ROTC scholarship up there in 1956, my first year of high school.

man kept Chihuahua dogs and you would find dog poop on the magazines sometimes. Abilene was a high-class place in those days. Said bookstore, unfortunately, was in one of the original historic buildings on 3rd and Buckeye across from the Post Office and just north of the Union Pacific tracks.

Anyway, those were the days when I got the words to songs by Ricky Nelson, the Everly brothers, or maybe Marty Robbins. Many of the songs I thought were "country-pop" like "A White Sport Coat".

About the same time my brother Paul was traveling quite a bit for Ehrsam Mfg. in Enterprise, Kansas. One day he came home from Kansas City and brought me a classical guitar method book, not really knowing too much about it himself. The author was South African or Dutch, Van der something. I took to it like a duck to water and was delighted to use the finger technique for plucking instead of the pick. It seemed to coincide with Chet Atkins' style, at least a little bit, the little bit I could learn. At that point I began to spend hours listening to a couple of his records trying to imitate the sound, but without a whole lot of success. But I did pick up at least elementary classic technique and could soon play a version of "Malagueña" and a few others.

40

JIMMY GONZALES

Another good buddy, Jimmy Gonzales, was a pal from baseball days, sports in school and our common interest in pop music during the time I was beginning the guitar. This coincided with my beginning days in studying Spanish with our old school marm, Miss Albergard. Jimmy did not admit to knowing the language but did understand it when relatives spoke. At least that's what he told me. Mexican Americans in Central Kansas still were very much a minority group and the way out was to deny one's roots. Most came to Abilene and worked on construction or maintenance jobs on the railroads. Jimmy lived with his family in a tiny house near the corner of 5th and Brady. I would bicycle from the farm and would meet Jimmy at his house, and we went on our bicycles to summer baseball. We both were collecting baseball cards, those Tops cards inside a package of bubble gum and you got five cards, always wishing for a Mickey Mantle. But there was something else that Jimmy liked that made us good buddies as well – a tiny, 45 rpm record player and a big collection of records. He seemed to have them all – Elvis, the Platters, Ricky Nelson, the pop artists of the day. We used to sit in his kitchen and listen. I don't know where he got the money for them, I certainly didn't have it. Once again like many other friends, Jimmy was not a top-notch athlete, not good enough to make the first team or all-star team, so we meshed a bit on little league teams, and I had him out to the farm for games of pitch and catch.

41

LARRY ALTON

This makes me think of buddies and religion. Catholics were a minority group in the town; I think I once counted some twenty-seven different Protestant denominations in the local phone book. So, many of my friends were Baptist, Methodist, Presbyterian, Episcopalian, and a whole hodgepodge of what we would call "other churches" for a better name - River Brethren, Church of Christ, you name it.

One buddy, and a good one too, Larry Alton, used to razz me about the Catholics, constantly asking questions and forcing me to defend my faith, but certainly not in any educated or bookish way, we were only teenagers. Larry was a good buddy, one of the first who had a car. He had, I believe, an old Pontiac or Oldsmobile or maybe it was a Ford from the 40s, a jewel of a car. Larry was very heavy when he was a kid, in fact fat, and I am sure he suffered a lot from nicknames the kids would call him ("Fatso" etc.). But he had a heart of gold and had good upbringing. He would come out to the farm and we would play baseball or basketball up in the barn. I am trying to remember, but I think it was Larry that I taught to milk the old milk cow. He also was involved with sports through Jr. High and High school.

It just occurred to me I have been talking about an intellectually slow kid, a black kid, a Mexican and a heavy set kid others called names (and I was not any angel either), but I think there was something in my upbringing or the way I am that considered others, their beliefs and feelings, in a positive way. Maybe the fact we were just fair, a bit below average in sports, that was the reason we were buddies. I could indeed get along with almost everybody if given a chance.

A little bit different was Doug Eagleton, a good friend; his father was a salesman and district manager for a local store. He was a jokester and liked to rib me, I don't remember about what. We had our good and bad times and I can remember we must have irritated the hell out of each other off and on. But the good times come to mind. He came out as well and I can recall playing basketball in the barn. We played a lot of military games with forts set up in the hay and tin can and string "walkie-talkies". As I said, he was a bit of a scalawag; tears from laughter would come to my eyes when he would fart in Miss Albegard's Latin class. How she put up with us and we did not get kicked out, and how I ever settled down to become one of her prize students in Spanish a year or two later, I'll never know.

I am sure I am leaving some one out. Slim Rivers, the baseball buddy who took us to the hobo camp, was from the south side of town and took me out to the Smokey Hill River one time. I had a fear of the river and snakes and all for some reason, perhaps coming from Mom or Dad's warnings.

Kyle Slopes was a friend over the years. His mother was also my 4th grade teacher at Garfield grade school, one of my favorite teachers over the years. Kyle also had a car and did customizing and all. Frank Steps was a good buddy of his and Doug Eagleton, and we were all together off and on during high school years. Part of the reason was none of us was good enough to make the varsity sports teams, but we went to most of the out of town games. That's also when we first tried beer drinking and smoking. Neither the beer nor the smokes seemed harmful at the time, and life was a big game and adventure. The scare stories of cancer and smoking had not really become widespread by then; it was grown up to smoke, cool. I can say to my credit that I did not have the habit of either smoking or beer drinking in high school although we did a fair amount of each.

Luke Zimmerman was always around, but more with church or family life. Although there was a period in high school when I was much more with the buddies I have mentioned, this because Luke was good in athletics and was in a different crowd for all those activities, we still remained longtime friends. All the guys I mentioned were not on the school teams in high school, at least not on the varsity first teams. I never really thought about that then for I wasn't in with a "bad" group, but just a different one.

Mom had always said, "Be friendly to everyone, but figure out who are the bad guys and keep your distance. No sense courting trouble." And that's pretty much how it worked out.

Everybody I've talked about at one time or another was out to the farm, Luke more than anybody else. We used to have great basketball games in the haymow. And I played an awful lot alone. I can recall getting home from school, practically any time of year, even in freezing weather, and heading for the barn. I had my heroes in those days generally high scoring All - Americans: Dick Knostman of K-State the first, Clyde Lovelette of K.U., and Jerry West of West Virginia. I could make baskets from any part of the play area of the barn; you even had to learn to arch the ball over rafters for long shots. I had it rigged so I could stand on a bale of hay to do dunk shots like Wilt Chamberlain. I probably played more alone than with friends, so that's when the imagination would take over.

42

PRETEND GAMES

I've told about the pretend games when I went "hunting" up at the pond with the 22 single shot Springfield Rifle or 22 Special. But there were lots more. I guess I did have a good imagination, either that, or was easily bored. Most of it was when I was maybe 12 on up to 13 or 14 before high school.

There was one game in particular that I played alone that sticks in my memory as great fun, a sort of stick baseball. I was totally immersed in baseball in those years, maybe 1951- 1957, probably from about 11 to 16 years of age. I listened to the radio, bought baseball bubble gum cards (giving them all away about Jr.-Sr. Prom time in high school when interests had definitely turned to the girls), collected cards and of course played in the summers in little league.

At home I invented a fantasy game that was the greatest. At least I think I did, I know Luke Zimmerman played it too, I'm thinking it was his idea. I would stuff my jeans pants legs down into my white socks, this to be like the major leaguers looked, and wear my baseball hat. There was a place north of the barn, right beside the silo where I would stand at "home plate." The bat was a lath stick, the handle filed so it would be smooth to hold. The baseballs were small stones about the size of a marble that I would toss up into the air and hit with the stick. I learned to really cream the ball. I don't understand the principle of physics, but if you pulled it just right, you could almost double the distance traveled. A single was anywhere against the wall of the barn, a double on the tin roof either side of the driveway into the haymow, a triple on the top part of the roof, and naturally a home run was over the barn roof. I would play all summer long, hours at a time, wearing out lath sticks and having to hunt for pebbles to hit. I was Stan Musial, but mainly I was Mickey Mantle. There were no strikeouts, only game winning hits. I would set the scene just like the radio sports announcers, and inevitably, it would be the last of the 9th, two out, a three and two count, and "bam," over the barn roof.

I was a bit sheepish about the game, not the kind of thing you announced to adults or even to people not close friends, but I do remember talking to Luke about it. But mainly, it was for me, for all the years I was just a mediocre player, striking out too much and not ever making the "All - Star" team during summer play. Correction, I did make it once, kind of a last resort player. I will never forget because that was the only time growing up when I was issued a real baseball uniform. There is an old black and white picture which shows me in baggy pants and shirt; the uniform was flannel, just like the major leaguers, not the polyester or whatever they used later on. I wore white sweat socks instead of regular baseball socks, holding a glove and ready to play ball. I recall playing in one game as an all-star, going to bat with a bat with a hunk missing on one side. I hit a solid base hit to right field and got thrown out at first base! I can remember running down the first base line as though it were a dream, one of those nightmares where a monster is chasing you and you can't seem to run. So it was strictly a "good news," "bad news" situation. It really was like a nightmare because just a year to two later I became a respectable if not outstanding middle-distance runner and ran a 2:28 half mile in the state track meet. I may have that time off by a few seconds, but it was my best.

Baseball by the way was not all bad. I was a pretty good fielder and did get some base hits once in a while. The highlight of the career was an indeed spectacular catch I made of a potential home run Pablo Esteves hit over the fence. I backed up gradually on the ball, stuck my glove over the fence and got it. Fame is fleeting.

But my heart was not just in hitting. Another game that lasted all too short a time, this because I broke the "baseball," must have taken place in these same years. I don't remember where I ran across this, maybe in Duckwalls' Five and Dime Store. Here was the deal: there was a package you could buy with two baseballs made of hard Styrofoam, but the balls each had a tiny hole, maybe the size of a rivet, in one side. This allowed a seemingly unlimited variety of ways to throw the ball making it do exactly what the big-league pitchers did, or better I suspect. I pitched game after game, throwing the balls against the wooden door of the haymow, being Robin Roberts, Bobby Shantz, Allie Reynolds or Whitey Ford.

It was absolutely incredible, even by the standards of an imagination garnered from years of devotion to the big leaguers! You could make the ball curve a good two feet! I figured out how to vary the spin and make it curve another two feet in the opposite direction. I could throw a fast ball that would rise about a foot and a half, a drop that would fall the same, and an honest to god knuckler that would flutter all over the place. The fun I had!

Writing this when I'm 18, if I could find some baseballs like that again, I would be out throwing them against a wooden fence right now. Once again, the game scenario was always the most dramatic – World Series, final game, but I always pitched no-hitters, now striking out the same guys I used to be when I smacked rocks over the barn roof. The end of the story is that I finally battered the two Styrofoam balls to death against the wooden door. I ask myself: where are they today? Why doesn't somebody make them again? Do the little kids know what they are missing? It's worthy of note that when playing "real" baseball, I tried and tried to throw a curve, and it never happened. So make-believe was much nicer than real life, don't ever let them tell you any different.

A variation of the pitching game took place outside the barn in the wide space between it and the farmhouse. There were three old rickety wooden windows on the east side of the barn; I used to spend hours pitching all sorts of small rocks against them, once again in game situations, striking out the best. But this time I had to develop some control, at least I had to hit the window for it to be a strike. I had the good sense to stick to smaller rocks. But this pitcher did not turn into a country "phe-nom."

I used to love to climb, yet crazily enough was scared to death of heights. I climbed every possible tree around the house and barn yard, climbed the steel steps all the way to the top of the silo for my "army scout" game, and walked to the top of the hill to spy over the entire area. But once I got myself into a scrape - I climbed up onto the tin roof of the barn on an old, rickety ladder and was afraid to come down (this must be what cats feel like in trees). I must have sat up there for two hours before I got the courage to test the old ladder once more. But once down, I never tried it again.

Talking about heights -the best-paying job I ever had as a boy in Abilene, one of the few times I was not doing farm work, was as part of a construction cleanup crew at a gas booster plant near Enterprise. My job, among other things, was to perch high up on a ladder to wash the dozens of windows in the place. I did not last long; there always seemed to be a stiff wind making the ladder sway, and all there was below were a steel catwalk and lots of machinery. I was terrified.

I'm sure there were many, many other games, a few of which I have described. I know playing "cowboy" was the favorite of earlier years, and I think my all-time favorite Christmas gift as a child was a gun and holster set, this in the days of seeing the Western B movies and Roy Rogers at the local cinema.

43

THE MOVIES AND OLD ABILENE

One of the entertainments that were popular in Abilene in the 1940s and early 1950s prior to television was the movie theater. The old Plaza Theater played an important role, and to a lesser extent the Lyric Theater, a poor cousin, an inferior house with little or no decoration, small screen, and black and white films. I can remember literally falling out of my seat laughing with my buddy Luke Zimmerman at films such as "Francis in the Army," Jerry Lewis and Dean Martin films, Ma and Pa Kettle movies and the Harlem Globetrotter story, all these at the Lyric. The seats were wooden with an assortment of chewing gum on the bottom, but the price of admission was right, 14 cents admission for children.

We truly passed through the period of the Saturday afternoon matinee and the golden age of the cowboy movies. First of all, even for poor or middle-class families it was little or no hardship to attend. Admittance was for the grand total of fourteen cents. My Dad would give me a quarter dollar and with the other eleven cents I could get a nickel bag of popcorn, or a nickel package of Milk Duds, have a nickel coke or root beer after the movie and still have a penny left over for bubble gum or a root beer barrel. I think there was a time when the quarter represented my week's allowance, but that's foggy now. It amazed me years later to see how long the theater maintained the price at that level or just a bit higher, and, evidently still made money for the two Stanfield brothers who owned both movie houses. I think adults paid 35 or 50 cents admission.

The movies were I suppose like anywhere else in the U.S. small towns at that time. Each session screened a few advertisements, the newsreel of national or international news, a great and it seems to me today truly funny and creative cartoon (Walter Lantz, "Loony Tunes", Disney), previews of coming attractions and finally the feature presentation. My years were a bit late for the Saturday serials although I have vague recollections of them. What I do recall is becoming an expert in my time on the movie cowboys. We had them all and continuous films of each. All of this now seems to be a sort of fantasy age, golden age to me now for it coincided perfectly with vintage Mickey Mantle baseball cards and Blackhawk and Superman comic books.

There was Hopalong Cassady, a grey immanence dressed in black and riding a white horse; he came to Abilene one time for rodeo and rode that horse in a parade on main street; Lash Larue, a B-film type but one who could handle himself and had a nasty bullwhip to settle with varmints, sidewinders and others of their ilk. The Lone Ranger and Tonto were around, but not much; they were much more popular as a serial on television in the mid-1950s. Tim Holt was still in some films; Tom Mix had pretty much gone by the way. A favorite of mine was the Durango Kid played by a Charles Stuart, a fellow who had to make a quick change from local citizen to super good guy and bandit chaser. I believe the ever-present Smiley Burnett was a regular as the sidekick and funny man. Gabby Hayes was around too, talking through his whiskers to his friend Roy Rogers, but this was a higher budget western.

Two movie-cowboys who remained a notch above the B films of the times were Gene Autry and Roy Rogers, the latter gradually winning out with color films, music, etc. "Back in the saddle again" and Champion were good, but Trigger, Dale Evans and razzmatazz won out for Roy. And there even was a dog, a German Shepherd I think, or was it a Lassie type? Gene's films were more often in black and white while Roy spent more money. His was a semi-modern scene on the ranch, with one of those genuine wood paneled station wagons that used to be the standard thing.

I remember scenes as though it were yesterday, particularly from the B movies: terrific shootouts where the guns rarely or never needed to be reloaded, bullets ricocheting off huge boulders, and lots and lots of fistfights. Stagecoach robberies were big, long chases were involved; and there was always the run-away carriage or wagon with the heroine saved by the cowboy who jumped from his horse to the wild stagecoach horse or into the wagon seat and grabbing the reins to gradually slow it all down.

I think these movies ended with a song. The villains dressed like businessmen with suits and string ties; they sported thin mustaches and spoke good, standard, American English, not that of the "cowboy." For a ten-year-old, what really stood out were the six- guns, the fancier the better; Roy's and Gene's had pearl handles; the villains in these movies all had dark wooden handles. I developed a fairly good trivia mindset seeing so many of the character or minor actors in other films later on, actors like Chill Wills or Andy Devine. Later on, now in my teenage years, the westerns were dominated by John Wayne or even Paul Newman ("Hud"); Jimmy Stewart in "Winchester 73" was a favorite too. There were many, many more, but their titles escape me now.

I have tried to recall exactly when puberty came and beautiful girls in the films began to draw more interest than the old "shoot 'em ups." I am sure it must have been early junior high or high school years. I can't place a specific film, but I noticed I did not mind the love scenes so much, in those days hugging and a passionate kiss, and in fact looked forward to them. I can remember Ester Williams in her swimsuits, Doris Day and a particularly young and sultry Liz Taylor in a white swimsuit in "Suddenly Last Summer." "South Pacific" and the Polynesian beauties and Mitzi Gaynor I think were part of it all too.

I can only recall one movie giving me nightmares, one of the early versions of "King Kong" on one of those Saturday afternoons. The nightmares were horrible and lasted several nights. Also wild animals, jaguars, black panthers and the like were a particularly scary thing. I can remember one Tarzan movie when he tackled what must have been a two-foot wide tarantula. And crocodiles and boa constrictors were the norm. I had the creeps for weeks. Then there were the original monsters like Frankenstein, the werewolf and vampires with Lon Chaney staring at the moon.

The movies were just an occasional thing for Mom and Dad. (Mom's favorite was "The Egg and I.") I have vivid memories of Saturday nights in the summertime, people in town at early evening to finish shopping or "trading" as my Dad called it. The local merchants would stay open later on Saturday night. Some folks would take in an early movie or would stay outside talking while the kids were at the theater. There were still iron rails in front of most of the downtown buildings, a throwback to hitching rails I am told. You could sit on the top one and just watch life go on by; I can recall being perched on one while listening to Dad pass the time with another farmer in town for the evening, or sometimes sitting in the back seat of the car, windows down, while Mom talked to an acquaintance from the front seat. As I think about it, Mom and Dad did not really go that much to the movies but would do the visiting while waiting for the early show to get out. I can recall climbing into the back seat after a movie and be asleep before we had gone three blocks; I guess Dad must have carried me into the farmhouse all those times. Don't know if I ever thanked him.

I don't really have the details on the buildings in town in the mid or late 1940s, but Abilene was founded about 1869, a terminal for the Union Pacific Railroad and an important shipping point for the cattle industry of the times. The Chisholm Trail from Texas to the rail point was the main reason the town became so famous in its day. The Belle Springs Creamery, incidentally of Ike Eisenhower days where he worked in the ice house, had been a drovers' cottage for the cowboys and the streets south of the U.P. tracks, A Street among them, were renowned for taverns where cowboys and prostitutes and gamblers and other varmints could be found.

From that beginning farming began and dominates yet today. The population of Abilene changed little in those years fluctuating I believe from five to seven thousand people.

I do remember the old "Toothpick" building on south 2ⁿᵈ Street that dated from the earliest days of Abilene. Like many other buildings it had the very high tin ceilings inside and ventilator fans. I recall old barber shops, dry goods stores (Pinkhams, Hamburgs, maybe J. C. Penneys), real drugstores with a soda fountain and accompanying furniture. Architecture in Abilene was Victorian with many beautiful homes, most of them wood frame, but a few of native rock or stone, Elm lined streets were many, altogether a pleasant place. Brick was used to a great extent on the commercial buildings downtown, but wood frame was the rule in residential housing. I know all this from rides into town and around in the car, but mainly from bicycle rides to church or summer baseball.

There was a blacksmith shop or two, the RHV feed store, hardware store, appliance store, shoe store, clothing store and grocery store. They in fact had "company" money that you were paid in from bringing in produce and could spend at any of their stores. Several brothers ran the outfit. It was the nearest thing we ever had to the old general store concept.

Got a little sidetracked here, but my idea was the movies.

44

HOLIDAYS AND THE FIRST DANCE

Holidays, religious holidays and the like were a big part of our days on the farm. One Christmas, all of us kids got Scarlet Fever and had to be quarantined at home. They moved a big bed down to the living room, and card table so Joe, Caitlin and me (and even Paul) spent most of school vacation playing Monopoly. It was one of the best Christmases I ever had.

Christmas was also a time for all that candy and Santa Claus. There were two separate events, the first sponsored by the Elks at, once again, the old city auditorium. It was jam packed with all us kids and some parents. Faded memories, but there always was a short show, and I think it was an annual event for some local tap-dancing school to bring in all the kids to perform. Tap Dancing was not for me or anyone I knew. But I recall one older kid who hauled his marimba out on stage to perform. But we put up with it all because at the end, the Elks would hand out these great sacks of candy. I recall the peppermint sticks, chocolates with mint inside, lots of peanuts, and to make everything all right, an orange or apple. But the big event was the arrival of Santa Claus himself in his "sleigh." We attended this event for many years, and I daresay it contributed, along with Halloween trick or treat and Easter eggs to a mouthful of cavities and silver fillings.

But the Catholics were to not to be outdone. At about the same time as the Elks event, in the basement of old St. Andrew's church there were more bags of candy and Santa Claus as well. I recall my Dad was both a member of the Elks (his forte' the Sunday afternoon gin rummy games) and the Knights of Columbus, so he was working both events. Great times. There was a "real" Santa Claus with red outfit, pillow under his shirt if needed, red cap with white fringe, black boots, and lots of "ho ho ho" was part of the deal. It was one of those times when us kids were playing "ping-pong" in a playroom to the side of the main room where the candy was to be giving out, just killing time. I had no ping-pong paddle so was using a glass jar to "catch" the ball; I slipped, fell, the jar broke, and must have cut a major vein. It took forever to get the blood stopped and the place cleaned up. Red for the season.

Another memory about Christmas, years later in high school was the Job's Daughters Dance. Prior to the dance there was a ceremony in the old Masonic hall downtown. Luke and my dates would sing perhaps "You'll never walk alone." We Catholics had to get special permission from the old Irish priest, Monsignor Fahey, to attend. It was grudgingly granted, and we seemed to survive just fine. No epic battles between Masons or Catholics, not that I knew even what a Mason was or Masonry meant in those days. Who cares? You go to the dance with a cute girl! Buddies who were Protestants were in DeMolay, the boys' version of Job's Daughters, but we never got around to talking about it.

But speaking of dances, I have to tell about the first dance and other stuff us guys had going on in those times, now shaving, hormones raging and the rest.

The First Dance. There are these moments of growing up essential to all my generation. My first dance was a junior high school dance. Good buddy Luke Zimmerman went with Kayla Scott and I with Sylvia Masserman (recall that her father was the junior high shop teacher). There was a "mother conspiracy" or perhaps better termed, just plain ole' dance planning. Mom and Sheila Zimmerman put their heads together to outfit us youngsters for the dance. I am pretty sure we were decked out in purple corduroy sport jackets, grey slacks, and I think a pink shirt. And a tie. What the reader needs to know is that we were at the height of Elvis Presley Mania during those days, and those I think were colors in style from him. There were corsages and all. And of course, we were chauffeured to the dance - no car 'mon' - by I think Mike's dad.

I can't remember the dance; we probably stood around a lot. But hormones were raging, and those "close" dances put pepper in the pepper can. I had a bit of puppy love thing going for Sylvia in those days, that is, until high school when an upper classman snatched her away; I think he had a car.

About this same time, we were going to dances at the Elks' club, I think maybe with Sylvia again, but who knows. But science and time march on. We eighth grade boys solved our "problem" - those close dances, cheek to cheek with those blooming young girls - or so we thought with a jock strap or athletic supporter under our shorts to ameliorate the problem. I guess we were "downsizing" before it became popular. Ah youth. Crazy, I don't remember the first time I kissed a girl, but I do know it was hot and heavy when I eventually got the old family car for dates in high school.

Back to Christmas. Main memories were at Church, and we always attended midnight Mass. Pretty sleepy when we got home, but no presents until morning. We had a real tree, decorated in a corner of the living room, and the presents under it. Mom and Dad and maybe Paul, Joe, and Caitlin did a good job; my presents were always a surprise. I never wished for "big" things like a bicycle (I inherited a repainted one from Joe). Presents were socks, maybe even underwear, maybe a pair of Dickie jeans or a flannel shirt. But a little kid remembers best the gun and holster set with the "pearl" handles just like Roy Rogers, or maybe the Red Ryder B-B gun. Christmas dinner might be ham, potatoes and gravy, but just as often was a big baked chicken, maybe a capon, but with Mom's good mashed potatoes, gravy, dressing and green beans. And maybe apple pie or chocolate cake for dessert.

Thanksgiving was the same food, mass in the morning, but best remembered after 1955 when we got black and white TV and watched football. It was always the Detroit Lions versus somebody; I remember Bobby Layne and Lou Groza, a place kicker. Must have been the Cleveland Browns. Everybody was home it seemed like, and there were big naps after the food.

Easter had a lot more memories. Brother Paul was big time involved in all that. He hid candy eggs down at the end of the lane for the Easter Bunny.

45

RADIO AND TELEVISION ON THE FARM

Radio was an integral part of growing up on the farm. I believe we listened most to the one in the kitchen, on the counter near the breakfast nook where we ate most of our meals except Sunday dinner. It made sense to have it there since Dad could catch his weather, agricultural and other news easily. At one time we had a model in the dining room that would be antique today: the kind set in a wooden cabinet shaped like the spade of a shovel, "Gothic" perhaps? Dad would thunder to all of us at the kitchen nook supper table, "Listen!! That's when we heard of Truman upsetting Dewey in the 1948 Presidential election (I was a tot and just remember the headline in the "Kansas City Star" the next morning). Sometime later, on those nights when we had the "score" of the dogfights in Korea with Saber and Thunderbird Jets versus the Russian Migs, there was the big announcement that President Truman fired General Macarthur because of him getting too big for his britches and wanting us to cross the Yalu in Korea and invade China.

I can recall in the winter sitting next to the furnace vent while listening to programs on that radio. I can also remember listening to baseball games in the summertime and especially to the Sunday afternoon programs while spread out on the floor in the upstairs bedrooms and listening to a different radio.

I believe it was high noon when all the farm news came; livestock reports, prices from the markets, and weather news. Associated with this was a music program. It was KSAL radio in Salina, Kansas, with a program I think was called the "Noontime Jamboree". It was evidently a poor takeoff on the Grand Ole' Opry type stuff. This show had some local talent, a couple of people "pickin' and singin'" and doing advertisements for feed for cattle, etc. The sponsor was the Gooch Feed Co. of Salina, Kansas, sponsor of the CK Ranch Annual Livestock Sale, a big event for me in my teen years. Each bag of Gooch feed had a red circle on it; you cut it out, saved it for the points on it, and when you had a few million or so could take those points and go to a beautiful ranch west of Salina and bid for real, honest to goodness livestock. I drove out one year with my friend Bob Gerson in our old green Dodge or Plymouth. I believe my parents sent me on my own; I can't recall how it came out, but I certainly did not come home with any livestock. I think I mainly wanted a chance at the free hot dogs and pop.

Anyway the "Noontime Jamboree" advertised hog feed, chicken feed, cattle feed and a special brand of "baby feed". There was a letter segment when listeners would write in with birthday requests. They would always sing the "Mom and Dad Waltz" for anniversaries and a corny, made up song for birthdays. There was a heavy dose of local 4-H and farm news with a full assortment of farm jargon, using words like "boar, sow, filly, barrow, steer, heifer" and such as needed. The program always closed with the religious section and hymn, often "Just a Closer Walk with Thee" and some good words to the wise.

There was another type of program, associated I think with the top 40 pop songs. I know I heard stuff like "Mockingbird Hill", "How Much Is That Doggy in the Window", "In a Pawn Shop, on a Corner, in Pittsburgh, Pennsylvania" and then in teen years what must have amounted to a combination of country, pop and very early rock and roll. I regularly bought a magazine for 25 cents that had all the lyrics of the songs and I would try to learn them on guitar.

Back to the farm and the radio. The favorite programs for me fit into two categories: the daily kids' programs from about 4:30 to 6:00 p. m. before the news, and the Sunday programs, afternoon and evening segments. The programs boiled down to "good" and "evil," heroes and villains and some fairly innocent humor. Sex was generally taboo, and violence was at least not the visual business of television to come. The daily radio programs of the 1950s were fantastic and I was a regular. I had lots of farm chores then, so these programs must have been worked in around them, can't say how.

I can recall, among others, "Straight Arrow," "Sergeant Preston of the Yukon," and "Bobby Benson and the B Bar B Riders". I swear there are even some episodes I recall, one of them a Chinese water torture with the drip, drip, drip and cries of pain, I think on Bobby Benson. The programs were a wonderful part of my life. I liked the music behind the action, the sound effects, but best of all was the gadgets you could send in for, this with 25 cents and a box top from Cheerios or Wheaties or Shredded Wheat. I was constantly sending in for the prizes, saving allowance money and begging my parents to do it. I received for instance the "Gold Nugget Straight Arrow Ring." It had a hole in it, and when you looked at it in the light you could see ... you guessed it, Straight Arrow's cave! Another one caused me no end of problems at school - trouble for me and several buddies who all ordered it. It was a "cannon" ring: you could make spit balls, pull back the trigger and "bam" - shoot the girlies. I cannot express the excitement the days I would take the school bus home, get off down the lane, walk up the lane and have the small package waiting for me on the kitchen table. It was heaven!

I don't think it was related to the kids' programs, but evidently a little later on when I began to be interested in music, we could get a country music or gospel station from Del Rio, Texas. It seems like the transmitter was in Mexico, thus they had super wattage and could be heard to the

Canadian line. They advertised a harmonica for just one box top and maybe 75 cents or a dollar. Life's tricks and deceptions hit home hard: the harmonica, when it finally arrived, was plastic and worthless. That may have been the end of radio merchandise and promises for me.

Sundays were the best for the radio programs, especially Sunday afternoon which was a delight: the crime programs, the mystery programs and some very, very scary shows. I recall the "Shadow" with "Who knows what evil lurks in the hearts of men?" and the laugh. There was "Gangbusters" and a couple of private eye shows, "Nick Reynolds" maybe or "Nick Carter," who knows. Man, but were they fun. I can remember Caitlin and Joe listening sometimes, but my listening companions were more likely buddies I would invite over on Sunday p.m. The radio was interspersed with all kinds of sports activities or playing outside.

But the best is for last: the Sunday evening and night programs with comedy shows: the "Jack Benny Radio Show" and "Amos and Andy." And we often heard the Edgar Bergen show with Charlie McCarthy and Mortimer Snerd. The sound effects of radio were absolutely magnificent, particularly on the Jack Benny show (the long trips to his vault with all the closing doors, footsteps, etc.) I recall many of the crazy secondary characters voiced by Mel Blanc: Si, the Mexican Benny would run into in the train station going to Cucamonga, Benny's old Model-T, Rochester, Mary Livingston, Dennis Day and the "yeeeeeeeeesss" salesman. What writers Benny had! We would see him later on television, and the show was good, but the joy of radio with its singular dimension of sound and the fact that we did the imagining and describing of the characters and scenes, these made it my favorite.

I can recall so well my disillusionment seeing "Superman" on TV in the 50s and also "Amos and Andy" after the radio shows. I first saw TV at Spencer Gallagher's house up on north Buckeye, almost outside the city limits. The Gallaghers had a small six- or seven-inch screen; the program was "Amos and Andy." Spencer's Dad also kept a pop cooler with big bottles of RC Cola; he charged a nickel to customers at his car repair shop, but they were free to us of course, I was in paradise. I can also remember seeing wrestling, a staple of early TV and my first trip into Kansas City with brother Paul and Mom where I stared at some big band program while we were in a restaurant. It was a whole new world, marvelous and mysterious.

One final memory from the radio days: listening to the Mutual Game of the Week baseball game on Saturday or Sunday afternoons. I have this vague memory of listening to the Yankees, my favorite team growing up, Mickey Mantle the greatest of heroes, when Mantle and Joe Dimaggio were both in the same outfield, 1951, I think. Mantle was first injured about that time, stepping in a drain in the outfield, and that seemed to be just the start of a long series of ups and downs for him and me. It really was the first in a series of tragic injuries that many say curtailed his career and greatness. But the ballgames came alive for me. I think all the baseball heroes of my youth: Mantle, Mays, Ted Williams, Stan Musial, all topped out at around one hundred thousand dollars per year.

We did not get television until 1955, a momentous day when my brother Paul brought home a black and white set from an appliance store in Enterprise, Kansas, where he worked at a local small manufacturing plant. And there was also a very tall antenna that had to be attached to the roof in order to pick up signals from far away Hutchinson, Wichita or perhaps Topeka; Kansas City was too far to pick up anything. Stations were also far enough away so that "rabbit ears" were of no use. Even with the antenna we could receive only three stations, and one of those was marginal.

Television and Baseball: the mid-1950s. There was a game of the week and for years I saw it off and on while growing up. For some reason Dad and Mom would let me see it and put off going to the field for some kind of farm work. Early announcers were Dizzy Dean and Pee Wee Reese. Then the trout fisherman from Montana, Curt Gowdy, Joe Garagiola, Tony Kubek (whom I saw walk into the Katz Drugstore on 12th and Main in Kansas City, Missouri, across from the Mühlbach Hotel with Moose Skowron and about dropped over with delight. This was approximately

1955 when brother Paul used company tickets to take some friends and me to my first ever major league game). I still remember Dizzy singing the "Wabash Cannonball" each ball game and all his braggadocio; I never minded because he was such a legend and was really sorry when he lost the job.

I can also remember other great ballgames, the time Mantle hit the ball over the roof at Briggs Stadium in Detroit, the All-Star game that went into extra innings and Stan Musial won it with a homer, maybe Harry The Cat Breechen who pitched a 13 inning no hitter and lost, but mainly I remember the Yankee Games. The New York market ran TV and success made the Yankees by far the most televised team. In the later 50s we watched pro football, but it was baseball that enthralled when we first got television.

Other shows. I can recall only vaguely but the fifteen-minute Perry Como show was a favorite; he walked out and sang; that was it, no falderal. We also watched another 15-minute show with a magician and comedian named Johnny Carson. I think I saw Jack Parr once in a while, but it was Steve Allen in the late-night slots, along with his sidekicks Don Knotts and the "man on the street" routines that I recall best.

The Honeymooners. This was the favorite on Saturday nights for years with Jackie Gleason, the fat bus driver, Art Carney his sidekick the sewer worker, and Audrey Meadows, the wise, suffering wife. With all these shows I remember the advertising for cars, the only time in my life when I could recognize the models, etc. Ed Sullivan advertised Mercury for years. Th e commercials actually talked about traits of the cars, their selling points.

The old G.E. Theater was another program we regularly saw on Sunday nights. I can recall a show when Burl Ives played a hangman who would sing a ditty or two. There was the highbrow "Odyssey" on Sunday afternoons with Alistair Cook with dramatized moments of history, like the death of Socrates. There was a lot more live drama on TV than now. "I Love Lucy" as well.

But the most watched show was Sunday night, the "Ed Sullivan" variety show: the Englishman who did the "passing out" ceremony; Señor Wences and his puppet in the box; the man who brought a chair out on stage and began laughing and by the time it was over we all were in tears and our stomachs hurt. And of course there were the first appearances of Elvis Presley.

So entertainment in Abilene for us was the weekly movie on Saturday, almost daily radio in its times, TV, and going to a local 4-H play or school function. The basic pattern began to change when I began to date seriously, this in the very late 50s, maybe a junior in high school. Drive-in movies, inside movies, high school sports, and lots of dances took up our time. In the summertime when I didn't have a date, we used to go out to Eisenhower park and play basketball or even tennis at times.

A funny memory: I remember we played golf during one phase of high school, not at the country club, but rather at a country course out south of town, renting clubs, and playing on sand greens and dodging cow pies in the fields. But a favorite summertime thing, from junior year on was when my old music buddy, Jeremiah Watson (guitar) and Loren Beasley (bongo drums) and I would go out to the park, maybe in front of the old bandstand, drink beer and play music. One night Luke Zimmerman and his cousin Jake joined us; and we had great fun with the music. More than once the police would drive by and tell us to pipe down. But never was there the slightest troublemaking or vandalism, nor were we bothered by others. I can remember the cool night breezes and laid-back times.

46

GROWING UP CATHOLIC

If I'm saying so much about this, it's because it's important. The O'Brien – Ryan family is of one hundred per cent Irish background, and the Catholic religion that goes with it was maintained by Mom and Dad. Dad's family was of course Catholic, but he never talked about specific Catholic memories. I know many of his brothers and sisters left the faith. I am not entirely sure why with the exception of Uncle Tim who left because of some mistreatment by the obstinate, old-time Irish priest in Abilene, Father Fahey. Result: not only Tim's own numerous children were lost to the faith, but all the grandchildren and generations to come. There were probably two sides to the story.

Mom had more education than Dad and spent a few years at the Catholic High School in Salina, Kansas, Sacred Heart Academy. She was the one who verbalized Catholicism more and was responsible for getting us kids to church. But Catholic tradition was equally shared by Dad. He had become a Knight of Columbus at an early age and had taken one of the advanced degrees. I remember the "Napoleon" style hat with the feathers and the cape, both smelled of mothballs stored upstairs, and especially the sword. I loved to play with the sword. Dad led a life of constant service in the parish, taking up the collection, doing carpentry work, volunteer work with the Knights and later on at the grade school, and in his last years constantly helped as pall bearer at funerals. He was never without his rosary at mass.

Mom had all her support activities as well, the Altar Society which helped to clean and prepare the church for mass, the D of I's, Daughters of Isabella, whose exact function I am not sure of. There were St. Joseph nuns who would come from Salina to teach catechism and summer school. We also did have the Missions during Lent by the guest priest, usually a Jesuit from the city, and a bit of fire and brimstone along with it. But what I'm getting at is that Mom, being more educated, probably verbalized more aspects of "Church", but Dad was no less a practitioner of the faith. Both had what I judge what a very deep faith; I never heard it doubted by either of them in our presence, and I truly believe they doubted little, or if they did, they kept it to themselves. The faith was largely uneducated on their part, a result of tradition and practice and not of any formal study on any advanced level.

But their faith was so important as a part of their lives; you cannot really separate who they were from what they believed and how they lived it out. We were taught to never lie under any circumstances, to "be good," and it had such an effect on me that I honestly believe that I could not possibly choose to do otherwise without the incredible guilt trip it would put upon me. One of my buddies said, "Yeah, O'Brien. He's so good he'll probably help a little old lady across the street, and she'll stab him with her umbrella."

Sunday Mass. We never but never missed Mass on Sunday or a Holy Day. I do remember discussion about missing on those few occasions we were traveling. I can remember stopping at churches in tiny towns in Western Kansas on the way to Colorado, even for what Mom called a "visit." There were times I would wish for a blizzard or some other act of God so I could stay home.

Snow was a good excuse since we had to get down the graveled lane and about two miles on asphalt to church. Due primarily to farm routine, I cannot recall anyone going to daily mass as a regular routine over the years, but there was an effort at daily mass during Lent. But rarely did we miss an evening service such as Benediction, Rosary or Way of the Cross.

The church was built I think in 1916 of a dark brick with a single bell tower and one long nave. The original altar was marble I think, of the style with niches for all the saints, and a crucifix in the center above the tabernacle, a truly mysterious place lined with velvet cloth and perhaps gold walls, where the Holy Eucharist was kept. There was a choir loft, a tiny "crying room" added later but seldom used and a baptismal font in the back. I spent a lot of time in the sacristy as an altar boy, but that's another story for later.

It was a country parish, or better, a small-town parish, and each family chose its place to sit and never varied from it. I believe that custom never changed in my eighteen years in town, and I imagine a place in the pew is often passed on to the children. I can recall that very few people would sit in the first two or three rows; I always thought they were either those who had contributed more or "extra pious" types who just wanted to be closer to the altar. The pews were of a dark hardwood, and there were padded kneelers. I can remember how my mind would wander during church, I had a way of losing myself at night staring at the candles flickering and thinking of who knows what. Funny, but certain images stick with you: one is of my Dad's hands, workers' hands with freckles or moles on them, but with a rosary.

Dad, once again, was firm in his beliefs and did not ever say too much, but he was exemplary in his actions. Rarely would I hear him swear and cannot really ever recall attacks on others, verbal or otherwise. There was absolute honesty in all dealings.

There is a scene etched in my memory. Of cold, cold nights in winter and Mom at home before bedtime huddled into the corner of the dining room with her feet in front of one of the furnace registers, saying the rosary. She often recalled the promises to Bernadette, Fatima and all, and she believed very much in the saying of the Rosary to avoid the victory of communism in the world. This, I think, was again as a result of one of the apparitions of the Virgin at Fatima. Mom also believed deeply in the protection of Mary at the hour of death. Our family said the Rosary regularly together. As a little boy I mumbled and rattled off all the prayers, it was so hard to concentrate.

Along with this custom was that of the scapular medals and others. It is all vague to me now, but we were urged to wear a medal of some kind since childhood. I can recall so vividly our old tarnished St. Christopher medal in the car. It was in the old Buick in the wreck of 1949, and I do believe that my surviving was in part in answer to prayer; who knows, maybe the medal had to do with it also. I can recall some embarrassment at wearing the cloth scapular to school and always preferred the regular metal medals.

Weekly confession. Another custom was almost weekly confession, generally on a Saturday afternoon. The family was in town anyway for shopping or "trading" as Dad liked to call it and then there was the afternoon matinee movie. Diverse memories come from that. I can recall a detailed picture of the confessional itself: the carved wooden outside, the darkness inside, the screen between me and the priest, the kneeler. We experienced three or four priests growing up in my time, but most dominant was of course Monsignor Fahey, the old Irishman. I can recall how quiet it would be in the church, how even a whisper seemed to carry far beyond the confessional, and the how the priest seemed to talk in a very loud voice when admonishing me to sin no more and do the penance. Confession was simply not a positive thing. The worst was that I seemed to commit the same sins day after day, week after week, yet felt obliged to confess again and again.

But there was no discussion about going or not going to confession; it was a stated fact and that was all there was to it. Of course, we were all taught in those days you would burn in the fires of hell for eternity if you sinned seriously and did not confess it. But there was another side to it. I recall the solitude, the peace and the quiet joy of sitting in the church on those quiet Saturday afternoons. The church had huge stained-glass windows and truly the brilliant late afternoon sun would create an atmosphere of beauty in the church. More than that was the absolutely unique feeling of having gone through the torture of admitting once again one's faults, getting up the courage to confess them and the absolute feeling of relief of being "clean" once again, the feeling you had a direct ticket to heaven should something happen to you. I do not know if that in any way was outweighed by the incredible guilt we carried with us much of the time. I do know the heavy weight that would fall on me later in the week when I would sin again and feel unsafe until the next confession. There was always the Catholic "out" of the "perfect" Act of Contrition, but you could not bet on it. We had little experience of the God of love in those days; our God was forgiving but severe and never forgetful.

The penance in those days in Abilene was generally a few to a full rosary of "Our Father's" and "Hail Mary's". There could be no fudging on this in my mind because HE knew. This however did not keep me from rattling the prayers of penance off as fast as I could and get the heck out of there. But it was a sort of Catholic magic; just saying the prayers seemed to make it all well. That is, until the next heavy date as a teenager when one was once again faced with the "near occasion" of sin. I can rarely recall any penance of dealing with people; we just prayed.

Holy Communion and First Communion. The Saturday confession was always followed by Sunday communion. But in those days as important as the communion was the fasting that went along with it. There were always rules to be followed. You absolutely could not eat anything from Midnight Saturday on. And you could not drink anything, even water, one hour before receiving. I can recall how precise we were on this, and that you had to get up early even to have a drink of water. There were prayers you said after communion, a set ritual I followed from the "Sunday Missal," some of them beautiful prayers, most I have forgotten. But there was no real "improvised" or personal prayer other than a "I'm sorry. Please make me do better."

We received First Communion at age seven, I think. Once again, we were prepared for it by the nuns in the two-week summer school held after classes in public school got out in late May, this since there was no Catholic school in town. Summer school was dreaded at first, but always turned out to be a lot of fun. And later on it kept me out of the fields and the farm work for an extra two weeks. It was held at the old Lincoln Grade School across from the church. In fact, this was the same school that was attended by Ike Eisenhower and his family who lived immediately across the street east from the school playground. The building was old, the steps were creaky and old, but highly polished oak I think. Desks were the old style with ink wells, a fixed top with a place underneath to put books. The seats were straight backed and were attached to the rest of the desk with a somewhat ornate iron grill framework, and several desks were attached to each other on runners. Memories are truly fuzzy of exactly what we learned to prepare for communion, but I know we practiced the actual routine with either unconsecrated hosts or candy or something to be sure we did it right. It was considered a grievous error by the nuns to allow the host to fall out of your mouth, and heaven forbid, land on the floor. I can remember several times as an altar boy when the host would fall off the paten and the priest would pick it up, crisis time. There was only one way to receive: with your eyes closed and your tongue stuck out, but not too far out.

I know we also had to memorize the "Act of Contrition" and practice going to confession. You had to be able to recite the sins, how many, how many times, how long ago you went to confession, a regular shopping list. I had a vague idea of Mortal and Venial sin; the latter should be confessed but it wouldn't "kill you" or make you burn in hell. But look out for the big ones, pain of eternal damnation if you did not "fess up." If you by any chance forgot a biggie, then you were obliged to tell it first thing next time, and not go to communion. Well, that was definitely a bad deal: all the family is sitting in the same pew, and only Mick does not get up to go to communion. Everybody knew he must have been up to something this last week. But in the case of venial sin you could go ahead and receive communion and confess it all later. It was all a bit legalistic.

Then there was that mysterious idea that we actually were receiving the body and blood of Jesus. I had quite a problem with that. That great big word "trans-substantiation" eliminated that problem since you did not have to think about "body" or "blood" or cannibalism anymore but you knew it was magically Jesus. I had a lot of difficulty with the hymns that talk of eating his body and drinking his blood. "Faith" was just a word then, but we got the idea that the water and wine were turned into the real Jesus, not just bread and wine with "Jesus" attributes. I always expected to feel different after receiving communion and guess I did upon occasion feel a bit "holier," but mainly I recall that a lot of times the host would not leave such a good taste in your mouth.

But "first communion" was a big event for us. The boys wore white shirts and ties, the girls pretty white dresses with veils. There are some old pictures with Joe's communion, but none of mine survived.

Confirmation. It also was a big thing. You were confirmed at about age twelve. I cannot remember exactly why it took place, but it was explained that you were in effect becoming a "Soldier of Christ." We were taught it was a renewal of baptismal vows, but since we did not remember those, I am afraid that part fell upon shallow soil. But I did have a vague idea it was a kind of growing up in the Church, of taking on more responsibility for one's actions and faith. The preparation was arduous. It consisted primarily in Catechism classes on Saturday mornings for several weeks and the drilling and grilling of questions by either the nuns from Salina or the priests, Monsignor Fahey Roach or later on Father Kramden. But great fear was once again instilled in us: on that special Sunday the Bishop would come from Salina to confirm us, there would be a public examination by him of all of us with the catechism questions. The fear of course was that we would be called upon in public (we knew almost everyone in the church) and not know the answer. And there was some vague idea that he would slap our face or something for some reason, to test us, during the process. Th e Bishop for me was a sort of mysterious dignitary from a faraway town who dressed like the Pope with the funny pointed hat and in scarlet. As it turned out, we knew or mumbled our way through most of the questions, no one got slapped hard, and we all got confirmed. I recall I did not feel much different after it was all over. I can't recall any special celebration at home either but am sure there must have been a treat or the like.

Religious Instruction. The main religious instruction outside the home was in the form of Saturday morning catechism. Since our town was small and there was not sufficient population or money to support a Catholic school, this was our only formal instruction expect for a mandatory two-week summer "Bible" school. I have lots of memories of summer school: the tremendous heat and sweat of playing baseball outside and then having to go in to attend classes in the un-air conditioned building, the great baseball games we would have, the picnic the last day, the nuns who were great hitters, nothing like that to gain our admiration, the beginning of puberty and girls. There were not that many kids, but the few classes were taught by St. Joseph nuns with the old-style habits, black and white, floor length, tiny crescent of face showing, not even their hair. We all wondered to ourselves, was it shaved when they became nuns? I thought so at one time. These were the real "nunerroonies" or "penguins." One class would be taught by Monsignor Fahey or the assistant pastor.

We hated Catechism for lots of reasons. Only Catholic kids had their Saturdays spoiled by having to go to church. Buddies played ball or whatever. But we had a compromise: arriving a half hour early and having softball games in the church parking lot. I recall the lessons were rote memorization from the famous "Baltimore Catechism." "Who is God?" "God loves me." "God is everywhere." "A sacrament is an outward sign instituted by God to give grace." You were expected to memorize the lesson for the week and then recite it when called upon in class. And after Catechism we would make a b-line on our bikes to summer baseball practice.

I remember Msgr. Fahey as both a smiling, lovable old man who talked funny and as a severe person who might slap a lazy or smart-alecky student. I can also recall Father Kramden, the young priest we all liked so much who was later chaplain for the Newman Club at Kansas State University. He was the only priest who ever seriously mentioned seminary to us when I was in high school. Funny. The priests were always forgiven for having big, nice and new cars. In those days gas was cheap, maybe twenty cents a gallon, so even at a priest's salary, $500 per year sticks in my mind, they could afford gas. Generally, the cars were donated by some heavyweights in the parish. And the priest did have to get around quite a lot, saying mass occasionally in little country towns with frequent trips to see the Bishop, etc. It was also frankly a reward for choosing that type of life, celibacy and all. Father Kramden on his day off would play golf, a hobby joked about by many in town, but not maliciously, but also a real extravagance for some of the old workaholic farm types in town. I recall him in his sporty golf hat, a big cigar and smile on his face. I have to admit that he was kind and a sort of hero to us, just what a young priest should be like. He more than once suggested seminary for me and Luke Zimmerman as well. But it was never pushed, and I never was inclined.

Monsignor Fahey on the other hand was quite elderly with a still huge white shock of hair, a friendly smile and the remains of an Irish brogue, this even after many, many years as a priest in Kansas. He was known for preaching not always so kindly from the pulpit. He once printed a list with all the families in the parish with respective dollar donations, something that would not be done today. But he was in charge and there was damned little anyone could do to protest. The standard joke was that once a year he would announce that he wanted to go back to Ireland "just one more time before I die" to see family, or maybe before "Mother" would die. I do not know the facts, but rumor had it that the parish would get together for a special collection for the one, last trip. He went to Ireland often. It was also known he appreciated a bottle of Scotch, the good kind.

Altar Boy. Like most of the young boys I also was trained to be an altar boy and to help serve mass. Father Kramden trained our group, and we did learn the Latin fairly well; it was memorized for response to the Priest in the mass. We actually understood very little of what was said but had the English translation like everyone else. I can recall Father Kramden's clear Latin during mass and Father Fahey's hurried and slurred version, not from speech defect or liquor, but years and years of hurrying through it. He would come into the sacristy and be dressing for mass and let out outrageous belches that of course caused us to fall into hysterical giggling. We giggled more in mass than you can imagine to the point of being scolded while still shaking with laughter. It was that time in life when anything could set us off - a belch, a fart, a funny look, whatever. And this included not only the daily mass with small attendance early in the morning, but the Sunday High masses as well. We wore long cassocks buttoned down the front from throat to knee, different colors according to the liturgical season, and white surplices on top. I guess we looked angelic enough. I can remember we were supposed to have our hair combed, and Bob Gerson came one day with hair oil dripping from his forehead. We heehawed over that. Shoes normally needed to be shined or we wore tennis shoes. Of course, someone would always trip over his cassock and something would go flying or be dropped.

It's all fuzzy now, but we took turns with the tasks of mass: one altar boy "got the book," that is, the mass book for scripture readings, one the paten for communion, both the wine and water cruets, towels and water for the priest's washing of hands after the offertory. The church had an old, beautiful, ornate, tall white marble altar. The steps were marble as well, and we had foam kneeling pads, but it still seemed nigh impossible to kneel through an entire mass. During the Consecration we were to climb up a step or two and hold the chasuble of the priest as he bent over to say the consecration prayers or genuflect. There was no pad on those steps, and it was killing. Oh, I forgot. Someone "got the bells" as well for ringing at crucial times throughout the canon of the mass. Each one of us would develop his own style of bell ringing, a big game. Other items were to prepare the incense for the incense boat that was used particularly on High Masses and on Holy Days. Inevitably we would choke and cough with the incense. Then there were the processions with the ciborium when we would hold a cross, candles or whatever. I think if I reread one of the old mass missals, much more would come back to me.

We alternated serving, each one of us would serve daily mass for one week, and three or four of us on Sundays which usually was a high mass sung by the choir, with Gregorian response, and the priest singing the mass, This was one of my most beautiful memories of those times. Our favorite time however was when mass was over, everything put away and our last duty was to take the empty water and wine cruets over to the priests' house and give them to the housekeeper, coincidentally also from Ireland. She always had wonderful bakery cookies for us, cookies of the most delicious and fancy kind. Anna, God bless her.

Before I go on to something else, I have some thoughts. For all the fooling around, the laughing and giggling, the making fun of Monsignor Fahey and his belching, farting and murdering the Latin, the experience was invaluable in my life. Sleepy, a bit groggy, I can recall the quietness of the daily mass, of that special moment of the Consecration, how special and close it felt to witness that special, magical moment, seeing the reflection of candlelight off the gold chalice (Father Kramden's had emeralds or rubies imbedded). I think then I believed in God.

There was a gift I did not realize for those few boys who were serving. There was a wooden altar rail that separated everyone else from the altar, from being so close to the actual celebration of the mass. There was the quiet closeness of the mystery of the presence of God during those moments.

Oh, I forgot the weddings. The altar boys always made a "tip" for serving at weddings, and I can remember one time when the time came for the wedding ring and they had forgotten it. We all just waited until they went and got it. Eventually they got hitched.

When I was smaller someone of course had to bring me to mass to serve, generally Mom. But later on I would actually ride the bicycle the entire way in from the farm to the south side of town where the church is. It was a fine thing in summertime.

Once we reached high school age there was an organization called CYO, Catholic Youth Organization. I am sure the idea was for additional Catholic teaching, but perhaps more so for socializing and keeping the Catholic kids together. I know the adrenalin and hormones were flowing in those days. We had all sorts of parties, dances mainly, and kids from neighboring towns would come. Now, there were just one or two what we generally perceived as good-looking Catholic girls in Abilene, so we ended up dating mainly the cute Protestant girls. But in a neighboring town of Chapman ten miles east of Abilene there was an unusually large Catholic population for its size, and the town was known for its rowdy and hard drinkers too. But there were some really cute girls. I can recall meeting one or two of them, liking them well enough, but nothing ever really coming from it, one reason being I had no dependable car of my own, another being I didn't want to have to get in fights with the local ruffians.

Th e CYO occasionally had conventions, and they were great fun. We went by car, bus and one or twice by train, a steam train at that! I can recall a crazy several-hour train trip from Abilene to Hays, Kansas. We all bought water guns before boarding, and the whole trip was a huge water fight. Can't remember a blessed thing about the actual convention, but the train trip was the best. An aside: that convention did involve one of my few early language experiences. I had an acquaintance from Abilene CYO named Weissman and we went to visit his grandmother in Hays who spoke only German, a great revelation to me.

To end all this a thought: I have always believed the part of the Bible that talks of the gifts of the Holy Spirit, that each has special talents. I often wonder why I never considered seriously the seminary, The time ripe for an early vocation would have been during or immediately after high school. Maybe just too much else going on. Just as well.

47

TIME MOVES ON, FARMING FOR DAD, HIGH SCHOOL AND GIRLS

Some of the things I've told you so far did take place in Junior High or High School, but as the time and years moved on to those years, there were some changes, and yet much was still the same. In the summers I still did farm work for Dad, part of a plan for paying for college I guess, the chores on the farm remained the same. After that first year in high school when Dad had to go to Florida to keep some money coming in and spent several months there, and Mom and I had the disaster with my 4-H pig project, when Dad arrived home, a couple of changes on the farm took place. Dad, seeing the inevitability of the future on the farm – lower crop prices, higher expenses to run the farm, and machinery wearing out, made a major change. He either rented out the cultivated land or did a share and share with neighbors or relatives to farm it. Financially it was a good move; he had less backbreaking working and came out ahead money wise. He kept that big vegetable garden on the north 40, and Mom her flower garden, so they still kept busy. And nothing changed at church, both Mom and Dad active at the parish.

The big changes came more with us kids. Caitlin was off to college on scholarship, the St. Joseph Nuns at Marymount, Joe with a naval ROTC full-ride to Marquette in Milwaukee, Paul full time at the manufacturing plant in Enterprise, doing a lot of traveling for the company, and me now at home alone with Mom and Dad. Puberty had come, more interest in the girls, more care to looking decent at school, and all that came with teenage years at the high school. During the school year I got a job at Gambles Appliance Store in town on Saturdays, but still had a full load of chores at home.

I've told about football and the concussion, mentioned running track in high school and the sports contests as a big part of social life. I was active in student government and even Student Council president for a year. There are only really two other things to talk about, the years in speech and Debate at High School, and, well, the girls.

I'll make it quick. I was on the Debate team for three years after the football concussion freshman year. I worked hard and played a bigger part each year. We had a terrific coach, Mr. Bock from the English section; we would make fun of his deep, melodious voice urging us on, "Now, fellows … ." We ended up winning the Kansas State Class A championship senior year, all a great experience. I think I mentioned I owned one suit of clothes, what I thought was quite elegant – a dark, striped, suit of clothes matched by a white shirt and tie – and that was the clothing for the occasion.

Studies went well, earning good grades, especially in Spanish class with the school marm marked by the annual Spanish banquet where I put on a Mexican vest on loan from brother Paul and played "Malagueña" on an electric guitar at the dinner. And I was inspired by the 4-H International Farm Youth Exchange speakers in Argentine gaucho outfits to go there some day.

So that leaves, puberty, girls, sex or the lack thereof up until Junior-Senor Prom. All us guys had heard stories about that being the big night to do it! Puberty had come in junior high, the hormones active, the juices starting to flow, shaving and the rest. Most of us guys were left to our own devices for sex, if you get my drift. I guess it was the times – still an age of innocence for most of us, church morality scaring us with the consequences of sin (I've talked plenty about that), and maybe more important, the consequences of real sex - you sure as hell didn't want to get a girl pregnant. Not much chance of that for most of us, and for sure in my case. I wouldn't have known what to do with it if I did have the chance. The stories of keeping a condom (we called them "rubbers") in your billfold, the stories of the "bad girls who put out," the "good" girls who were sometimes bad, and all was just pretty much talk. Folklore I'd say. I've said this before. It never happened to me. But what we called "extreme petting," lots of heat in the dark movie theater or the front seat (not the back in my case) of the car on "hot" dates, all this took place once I got to borrow the old family car for dates. If you got the girl's bra off or at least got your hands under it in the right place, that was nirvana.

I probably dated most of the available cuties in those four years, including a puppy love in town, driving out into the country for some girls, never "going steady," but it kind of culminated at senior-prom time senior year. You're thinking, "Aha! Mick got laid!" I might have wished that then, but no, my date was a real cutie-pie, temporarily available because her boy friend of the last three years was now away at college. It was almost puritanical – maybe a bit of cheek to cheek dancing, but once dinner and dance were over, she went to a slumber party with the senior girls and I went fishing and drank a bit of beer with buddies.

What was far more significant was a small event as we were decorating for the prom. A buddy had his car there, and his entire truck was full of boxes of baseball cards. We all were feeling generous, more interested in the boobs and buns of the girls, so several of us gave all our years-long collections of cards to the friend. Seemed an okay thing to do, not much emotion involved. I've heard of Moms just throwing them out when junior lost interest. But I thought about it later, maybe while on a tractor plowing for a neighbor. The card business was pretty stupid maybe, but water under the bridge. I'm thinking, indeed, a bridge to things to come.

That summer, my last before heading off to college in Kansas City (I had done the tests, the applications, and got a small scholarship to a

Jesuit School in Kansas City, a crazy connection with a lady friend of Mom's whose son went there). I worked 60 hours a week at the local ice plant, crushing ice in the icehouse for 30 lb. bags and doing the local town delivery route. At night I drank a lot of beer at ten cents for a small glass (a dollar meant a fun evening), and was beginning to get clothes, typewriter, Sears guitar and all ready for Kansas City. That was when it happened.

48

THEN IT HAPPENED

It was the middle of the summer, the day had been hot with those Kansas winds, I was baling hay for a neighbor, and had taken a bath to get the grime off, watched some TV and was early to bed. More work to do the next day. To this day I don't know why, maybe that ole' Catholic Guardian Angel or something, but I woke up in the late night, early morning, with a start. There was smoke in the air, coming from the hallway to downstairs. I threw on my jeans, a t-shirt and tennis shoes, and ran down the stairs, yelling, "Mom, Dad, there's a fire." Both jumped out of bed, still in their night clothes, Dad grabbed Mom, half carrying her, and ran into the front room, yelling, "It's in the kitchen and spreading out the back door!" We helped Mom through the front door, out on the porch, and down the steps. The heat and flames were behind us, intense, so no chance to do anything but run. All like in a dream. I just remember we three standing outside the front gate, watching the flames, Mom in tears, "Sean, Sean, what'll we do?" Me in shock.

Dad had managed to get his billfold and car keys, and was yelling at me, "Mick, get in the car to town and to the fire department!" The only telephone was inside the house, and it now was in flames. Before I could get to the car, the fire now engulfing the house, we heard the sirens and soon three firetrucks were roaring up the lane, including the hook and ladder. Somebody along the highway must have seen it and alerted the police and fire department in town. Abilene police cars and Highway Patrol were right behind the fire trucks. It all happened so quick I'm not sure of what and when, but one of the firemen said, "Sean, Molly, Mick. We're getting you to the hospital." Dad said, "I don't think we're hurt. Give us a minute."

I never had seen that before. Mom and Dad were holding tight to each other, staring up at the farmhouse, the roof now in flames, second story timbers crumbling to the ground, both crying, Dad trying to console her. "Molly, we've got insurance. That old house was falling down anyway. All our important stuff is in the safe deposit in town. I'll build you a new house with everything you ever wanted. Right here with a view to the lane. And we'll get new clothes in town. The main thing is we're safe, not hurt. It'll be all right. St. Christopher or a guardian angel, and maybe a little help from Mick, saved us." I moved over beside them and we all hugged. Now I was in tears. This was my whole life, the only home I ever knew. The fireman insisted, we all piled into a highway patrol car and were soon up at the hospital.

Friends from the neighborhood and church were already coming to the hospital. The Zimmermans lived just across the street and they were all there, Luke, his mom and dad. Luke's Mom said, "Thank God you're safe. We've got plenty of extra clothes, I'll have outfits for you all over here in just a few minutes." Doc Bernard had arrived, checked us all over and said, "Molly I'm keeping you over night. I'm giving you a sedative. You'll get some sleep and can face all this in the morning. Sean, Mick, I don't think you need to stay here, but maybe they can fix up beds for you in a room near Molly, just for tonight. Maybe that sedative's in order for you Sean and Mick too." I don't think Dad slept any that night, but they gave me a shot and I clunked out until morning.

It wasn't until later that morning that we were told that the same night Reverend Watson's church was broken into and basically totally ransacked. And that KKK was painted in red on the front wall of the church. The Watsons were not hurt but were shaken. They all came to visit us in the hospital, paying respects. And I guess sharing misfortunes. We would all only connect the dots between us and them days later. We didn't know it then, but later that same day when Dad and I went out to the farm to see what was left, the same red KKK was painted on the wooden post of the side gate to the house. And a message in red paint on the sidewalk up to the house, "Cat lickers and nigger lovers! This is a payback." They were so brazen they left the red gas cans on the ground by the gate. First mistake. When Dad told Mom, still on doctor's orders for bed rest that day in the hospital, she began to cry, and recalled her Mom Minnie telling her of those days in the 1920s when the Klan was active our west and Mr. Donnelly made the decision to sell the farm southwest of Solomon and move to Abilene, mainly for his family's safety.

We were all in shock, but the next few days were unforgettable. Paul, Joe and Caitlin had all arrived home, and we had a sad, but grateful reunion. What can I say? All just thankful to be alive and together.

The biggest act of kindness was from church. One of Dad's fellow Knights of Columbus had a furnished apartment house in town and said we could live there as long as needed until the new farmhouse was built. That would be several months, even after I would leave for college in Kansas City. I don't know if I talked about it, but Dad had been a member since the early 1930s and participated in annual charity events for the Knights for 30 years. All kinds of clothes, pots and pans and basic needs came out of nowhere it seemed, all helping us settle into the apartment house.

I guess it was then that Mom and Dad had some long discussions and began to evaluate the future. Caitlin had announced her engagement to Ron Schmidt and he and his brother had expressed interest in buying the farm. That together with the insurance would allow Mom and Dad to retire and settle into a small nice house near Eisenhower Park in town. I don't think it was an easy decision. Both Mom and Dad knew no other life than being on a farm. But Dad was getting older, too old for the demanding physical chores and tasks of being a farmer; the machinery was old and worn out, and crop prices were low. I think the saving grace was that they would keep the north 40 with the pond (the reader recalls, whittled down by the government in 1958 with the Interstate Highway cutting off 40 acres on the north edge of the farm), and Dad could still have his big vegetable garden and be out on the land. And that's what happened.

I said there was a good reason I'm writing this at eighteen. That's when it really all ended. I'm in college and it's going to be my senior paper when the time comes. If it comes to more than a 200-page typed manuscript, it won't matter 'cause it's my memory and our story.

EPILOGUE

There wasn't any such thing as a private detective in Abilene; if there had been, he would have starved to death from a lack of business other than adulterous men and women running around and divorces. But the police and some lawyer friends of Dad's from his long years of once-a-week gin rummy games at the Elks Club in town didn't let the matter rest. Those gas cans I mentioned were traced back to a sale at the local hardware store (I guess the KKK people weren't afraid of anything or anybody), and in just two months several arrests were made linking two separate families from west of town out between Sand Springs and Solomon. Two men and a teenager were arrested, charged with arson and second-degree attempted murder plus vandalism on the Watson church. The Dickinson County district attorney handled the case but had plenty of help from the lawyers. It never came to a jury trial, thank God, because Mom, Dad, me and the Watsons would have all had to face the criminals (we did all have to give affidavits in court).

Here's the kicker. It turns out they were all relatives of those scoundrels I mentioned before, of that event of three or four years back – the Enterprise Bank Robbery and the chase and shootings taken place after the bank robbers tried to kidnap me and use me as a hostage. The two men were the robbers' cousins and their son was the same redneck who had picked a fight with me and called me all those names in school just a few months back. And all sure enough were members of a KKK group out west of Solomon. I guess in their minds it was all revenge. All three were convicted and sent to Kansas State Prison in Lansing for a twenty-year term. And were told that the terms of parole, if they made it that far, would be never to step foot in Abilene or Dickinson County again and never contact in anyway the O'Briens or Watsons. The County Sheriff had their mug shots in a big poster on the county jail wall and said he'd never take it down.

It wasn't just the Catholics and the local Negroes who were up in arms. Nobody but nobody, regardless of religion or race, liked the Klan, town folks or farmers. I don't know exactly what happened or how, but names were dug up and about a dozen families moved out of the Sand Springs – Solomon area in the coming months. Where they went I don't know, but gossip had it that on up to Idaho or Montana with all the other "rugged individualists."

Mom and Dad both had always said that people are good; if you give them a chance, the best will come out. Whatever or however, merchants, carpenters and handymen in Abilene got materials together and at nights and on coming weekends not only remodeled Reverend Watson's church but basically rebuilt it and modernized the whole thing. There was an "open house" service when it was done, and history was made – whites and blacks in Abilene celebrated together, sang hymns and thanked the Good Lord for another day that day. "Amazing Grace" was the hymn of the day.

I won't and can't say I don't think about it. We could have all died. It's just been a few months ago. Mom and Dad have moved into that house by the park and are back to normal routine, Mom playing bridge with her church ladies, Dad active at church with the Knights (Reverend Kramden says he can always be counted on to be a pall bearer at funerals and never misses a rosary), on the farm at the garden, and still time at the Elks with the gin rummy cohorts. Caitlin and Ron are building the new farmhouse.

We all are moving on, but my memories and this story aren't going away, anywhere, anytime.

ABOUT THE AUTHOR

Mark Curran is a retired professor from Arizona State University where he worked from 1968 to 2011. He taught Spanish and Portuguese and their respective cultures. His research specialty was Brazil and its "popular poetry in verse" or the "literatura de cordel," and he has published many articles in research reviews and now some sixteen books related to the "cordel" in Brazil, the United States and Spain. Other books done during retirement are of either an autobiographic nature – "The Farm" or "Coming of Age with the Jesuits" - or reflect classes taught at ASU on Luso-Brazilian Civilization, Latin American Civilization or Spanish taught at ASU. The latter are in the series "Stories I Told My Students:" books on Brazil, Colombia, Guatemala, Mexico, Portugal and Spain. "Letters from Brazil" is an early experiment combining reporting and fiction, and "A Professor Takes to the Sea" is a chronicle of a retirement adventure with Lindblad Expeditions - National Geographic Explorer. "Letters from Brazil II" is a continued experiment in combining facts and fiction, but more fiction. Finally, "A Rural Odyssey – Living Can Be Dangerous" is more of the same.

Published Books

A Literatura de Cordel. Brasil. 1973

Jorge Amado e a Literatura de Cordel. Brasil. 1981

A Presença de Rodolfo Coelho Cavalcante na Moderna Literatura de Cordel. Brasil. 1987

La Literatura de Cordel – Antología Bilingüe – Español y Portugués. España. 1990

Cuíca de Santo Amaro Poeta-Repórter da Bahia. Brasil. 1991

História do Brasil em Cordel. Brasil. 1998

Cuíca de Santo Amaro – Controvérsia no Cordel. Brasil. 2000

Brazil's Folk-Popular Poetry – "a Literatura de Cordel" – a Bilingual Anthology in English and Portuguese. USA. 2010

The Farm – Growing Up in Abilene, Kansas, in the 1940s and the 1950s. USA. 2010

Retrato do Brasil em Cordel. Brasil. 2011

Coming of Age with the Jesuits. USA. 2012

Peripécias de um Pesquisador "Gringo" no Brasil nos Anos 1960 ou A Cata de Cordel" USA. 2012

Adventures of a 'Gringo' Researcher in Brazil in the 1960s or In Search of Cordel. USA. 2012

A Trip to Colombia – Highlights of Its Spanish Colonial Heritage. USA. 2013

Travel, Research and Teaching in Guatemala and Mexico – In Quest of the Pre-Columbian Heritage

    Volume I – Guatemala. 2013
    Volume II – Mexico. USA. 2013

A Portrait of Brazil in the Twentieth Century – The Universe of the "Literatura de Cordel." USA. 2013

Fifty Years of Research on Brazil – A Photographic Journey. USA. 2013

Relembrando - A Velha Literatura de Cordel e a Voz dos Poetas. USA. 2014

Aconteceu no Brasil – Crônicas de um Pesquisador Norte Americano no Brasil II, USA. 2015

It Happened in Brazil – Chronicles of a North American Researcher in Brazil II. USA, 2015

Diário de um Pesquisador Norte-Americano no Brasil III. USA, 2016

Diary of a North American Researcher in Brazil III. USA, 2016

Letters from Brazil. A Cultural-Historical Narrative Made Fiction. USA 2017.

A Professor Takes to the Sea – Learning the Ropes on the National Geographic Explorer.

    Volume I, "Epic South America" 2013 USA, 2018.
    Volume II, 2014 and "Atlantic Odyssey 108" 2016, USA, 2018

Letters from Brazil II – Research, Romance and Dark Days Ahead. USA, 2019.

A Rural Odyssey – Living Can Be Dangerous. USA, 2019.

Professor Curran lives in Mesa, Arizona, and spends part of the year in Colorado. He is married to Keah Runshang Curran and they have one daughter Kathleen who lives in Albuquerque, New Mexico, married to teacher Courtney Hinman in 2018. Her documentary film "Greening the Revolution" was presented most recently in the Sonoma Film Festival in

California, this after other festivals in Milan, Italy and New York City. Katie was named best female director in the Oaxaca Film Festival in Mexico.

The author's e-mail address is: profmark@asu.edu
His website address is: www.currancordelconnection.com